THE 1st HORROR SHORT STORY COLLECTION

BY
Jim Mullaney

Stories Never End

Contents

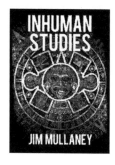

I think that every writer must have at least one short vampire tale in them, and, for better or worse, this is mine. Its tone is a little lighter than the other stories in the collection, as the hero of the piece learns that while the battle between good and evil may be eternal, sometimes it can be much more fun to go with the flow and simply give in to temptation.

1

Tom absently flicked through the pages of the book Professor Palmer had forced upon him earlier, not so much scanning the information on display as instantly disowning it. The subject matter was hardly to his taste in any case, but add to that the fact that this particular tome had been added to his course's reading list by a man he had learned over a period of two years to thoroughly despise and it all added up to an academic cocktail of an extremely tasteless nature.

I ask you, Tom thought to himself in disgust – *vampires*. Of all the bloody stupid things in the world, *vampires*...

In disgust, he threw his book aside and leaned back on his chair. The book's ridiculously lurid cover leered up at him from the pool of light cast by his desk lamp, and he found himself returning the gesture in kind, by giving the book the finger.

'*Vampires in History*,' he said aloud, 'what kind of Professor asks a serious archaeology student to read tripe like this?'

He groaned with despair and then reached for his cigarettes, still eyeing the book with disdain.

'You know what you and Palmer have in common?' he asked the book as he lit up. 'You're both completely full of bullshit.'

Tom exhaled a blue cloud of smoke from his nostrils, glancing out through the bedsitter's single window at the night, and then wearily reached for the textbook again. There was nothing he would have liked better than to bin the damn thing and get back to thinking about a subject far more interesting and closer to his heart – like his girlfriend Judy, for instance. However, he was well aware that Palmer would be asking questions soon, and he'd made it plain enough in the past that if Tom didn't play nicely, then he – Professor Rupert Noel Palmer – would take his bloody ball home, and Tom could forget about his degree.

There was no doubt about it, Palmer definitely had it in for him, just because Tom had shown his theories to be wrong a couple of times (and yes, okay, had also caught him cutting and pasting a few online articles and claiming the result as his own work), but it seemed there was nothing to be done about it – short of killing the egotistical, vindictive old bastard, that was.

Tom paused with the despised book half-open and his cigarette wedged between his lips as an image of Palmer, cold and rigid in a pool of his own jellified gore, passed marvellously through his mind.

'Oh, yes please,' Tom breathed. 'I could *really* go for that...'

Then he sighed and shook his head sadly.

'Pity wishes don't come true,' he said to himself. 'I'd love to wake up and find Palmer's mutilated corpse at the foot of my bed one of these days...'

2

Judy stepped out of the shower just as the last spurt of water fell from the showerhead. Hurriedly, she slip-slid over the tiled bathroom floor and sat down on the toilet, her eyes closing in blessed relief as her aching bladder – teased and encouraged by the shower water for the last ten minutes – finally got the chance to empty itself of the last few fluid ounces of alcohol from the previous night's all-girl binge.

'Oh Jesus,' she moaned aloud, her hands going up to hold the sides of a head that still throbbed violently from an excess of frivolity and indulgence. The early morning light coming in through the window showered her with beams of light that felt like a mild distillation of acid. How many drinks did she have last night while she and Leila were getting ready to go out on the razz? How many did she have in the pub later? And how many *after* that in the nightclub? She vaguely recalled a bar lined up with ranks of shot glasses...

Too many, she decided. Far, far too many.

Judy blotted with a piece of toilet paper, then stood up and flushed the toilet. She took her towel from over the radiator and wrapped it about herself luxuriously, just like she'd seen them do in the movies – but the next moment she coughed hackingly and had to rebuke herself for smoking too much. She spat a bubble of phlegm into the toilet and grimaced at the taste. She didn't much feel like a movie-queen this morning, and she was pretty sure that she didn't look like one, either. Unless she was the movie-queen currently playing Dracula's daughter, that was.

Judy looked at herself in the mirror and frowned at the dark hollow circles beneath her eyes and – of this she was thoroughly ashamed – the large, vivid love-bite that had somehow manifested itself on her neck overnight. Just how this particularly adolescent scar had come into being, Judy had not the slightest idea, but she realised that high collars were going to be the fashion statement this week. Especially as she had a date with Tom tomorrow night, and Tom was notoriously a jealous pig.

If they ever stopped arguing long enough to make it to bed together, Judy would have to make sure that they made love in complete darkness. It wouldn't do for him to see the suck-mark on her neck. It would inevitably make him think of whatever she might have sucked in return, and then all hell would break loose.

There was a knock at the bathroom door and Judy heard Leila, her flatmate, asking if she wanted coffee. *Black* coffee.

'Please,' Judy responded, and then asked, 'How did I get this mark on my neck, Leila?'

'What mark?' the muffled voice asked back.

'My beautiful love-bite, the hickey from hell – how did it happen?'

4

The door opened and Leila leaned into the bathroom, the jacket buttons on the striped pyjamas she habitually wore to bed partially undone, revealing a chest as flat and featureless as the face she now turned on Judy. Her eyes, however, shone with an attractive humour.

'Don't you remember?' she asked, and a smile cracked her blank expression and revealed that she was, in fact, a very pretty girl indeed. Popular too, if the sheer number of her boyfriends was anything to go by. 'You seriously don't remember any of it?' she asked again, her smile now positively huge.

But this time, Judy was in no mood to be the object of her amusement. Blushing wildly, she turned on her friend with mock anger

'If I could *remember* what I got up to last night, I wouldn't be asking you, would I, you oversexed twig. Now tell me who's been sucking my neck before I push your head down the toilet.'

Instead of answering, Leila merely turned and walked away, through the living room and towards the kitchen. A dark chuckle bubbled up from her departing figure and her step became jaunty in the extreme.

'You wouldn't believe me if I told you,' she called back to an irate Judy. 'You just wouldn't believe me.'

'Why don't you try me?' Judy shouted back, her anger now not completely an act.

The only answer she received was more laughter, and she almost screamed in frustration, but was afraid that if she did so, her head would split in two. Instead she pulled the towel tighter about herself and then followed Leila into the kitchen, leaving a trail of wet footprints across the lounge carpet.

3

Palmer pulled over to the side of the road and parked the car close to a post-box, kerbing the wheels. He killed the engine and released his seatbelt, feeling a sour, feverish mist of perspiration swamping his whole body. Mopping his brow with his sleeve, he opened the VW's glove compartment and pulled out his half-finished bottle of Tequila. He unscrewed the bottle's cap and took a long, long swallow that burned his throat, made his head swim, and effectively neutralised any small chance he'd had of remaining sober today.

Sober? What was he thinking of? If things went as planned, he wouldn't be drawing another sober breath until the whole damn mess was over and done with, and if he was still *alive* by the time it was finished, and still in his right mind, then maybe he wouldn't want to draw a sober breath ever again.

However, if he wasn't so lucky and he had to pay the full price for dabbling in the supernatural...if he were to die...or worse...

'Stop it!' Palmer commanded himself angrily. 'I'm not going to die. For the good of us all, I must not die...'

He took another swig from his bottle – a slightly smaller measure this time – and winced in embarrassment when he saw a woman leading her small child away from the direction of his car, looking back over her shoulder, her face disapproving. She must have thought him insane, sitting in his badly parked car, necking alcohol at this time of the morning and shouting at himself. Probably he *was* insane, a little. You couldn't see the sort of things he'd seen just recently and stay completely in your right mind.

'Don't worry,' he whispered now. 'Don't you worry, Rupert, old boy, you're not going to fail...'

Palmer's eyes fell on the small, sealed Jiffy bag resting on the passenger seat. He picked it up and held it to his chest, almost cradling the padded bag like a baby.

'...but just in case,' he muttered, 'this will be my little insurance policy...and God help me if it's needed.'

Palmer stashed his bottle back in the glove compartment and then pushed open the VW's door, holding it wide with his foot while he clambered out. The effort made his head swim even more than it already was and he smiled drunkenly to himself. At least this way, he had a chance.

He staggered over to the post-box, ignoring the many disapproving glances that came his way. He had been on staff at the local university for almost twenty years now, and in that time he had made a lot of friends outside the halls of academia (although not too many *in* the halls, if he was truthful). Unfortunately for Palmer, most of them appeared to have chosen this moment to walk along the town's busy high street, and he had to make a point of avoiding eye-contact. He must have made a good job of looking like someone else, because not one person he knew tried to speak to him.

On the other hand, maybe they were just ignoring him the way that most people ignored an embarrassment. It really wasn't socially acceptable for a university Professor to be walking the streets – to be driving a car for Christ's sake – blind drunk at 9:15 in the morning.

Palmer dropped the Jiffy bag into the post-box and heard it hit bottom with a little thud. This confirmed his first thought that he'd missed a recent collection, but that wouldn't matter. If it turned out that the bag's contents were needed after all, they'd still be delivered in time.

Not in time to save his life, of course.

But maybe in time to avenge it.

4

The day had passed like a couple of bad days squeezed together for purposes of economy, and now Judy sat in the lounge bar of The Henry VIII, a public house that'd had Tudor pretentions of an almost epic quality since its expensive refitting earlier in the year. In fact, the only things spoiling the illusion were a quiz machine, the jukebox, and a series of day-glo signs advertising the pub's menu of special evenings. Karaoke nights, quiz nights, Thai nights, curry nights, and free Wi-Fi throughout.

It wasn't the most sophisticated meeting place Judy had ever attended, and, if the truth were told, she privately hated the place. If it weren't for the fact that it was Tom's closest – and therefore his favourite – watering hole, she wouldn't have stepped in through its doors for a king's ransom. As it was, she had little enough excitement in her life these days without alienating herself from the man who had been her lover for the last nine months or so. He wasn't exactly the nicest, most congenial boyfriend she'd ever had, but he could certainly be passionate, and passion was still a novelty in her life.

Judy glanced at her watch, wondering why Tom was so late. It was already ten minutes after the time they had arranged to meet, and for the majority of those ten minutes she had been getting a lot of very horny looks from a large group of male students who were propping up one end of the bar. The ringleader of this rampant gaggle had the figure of a rugby player and Judy could all but see the muscles rippling between his ears. He was still looking at her now, she saw, and his half-drunken leer was not a turn-on in the least.

She turned away and tried to think of better things; she tried to think about her course, which was going badly for her, but as usual the good thoughts just wouldn't come. Sooner or later she was going to have to face the painful, awful truth, which was that she simply wasn't any good at what she most wanted to do... But for the moment such admissions were banished. She would have none of them.

Next she passed on to Tom's problems, about the friction which existed between him and Professor Palmer, but even the *idea* of thinking about this wearied her beyond belief, because lately that was all the conversation Tom seemed to have. She found it hard to remember a single moment, apart from when they had sex, that Tom had ever said anything to her that was not Palmer-related.

It was a good job they had sex a lot.

'Let Tom work things out for himself,' she admonished herself. 'He's a big boy now. If he wants to be mothered, he can take the train to Norwich and do it for real.'

This constant jockeying of tedious thoughts for position in her weary mind made Judy unbearably tired, and so she tried instead to think of the only escapist detail of her life at the moment, which was the story – as told by Leila, the sexiest twig on the planet – of her horny, drunken escapades. It was a story of alcohol, debauchery, and more alcohol, but of these components, there was only one which interested Judy at the moment.

Leila had told her that in the nightclub – a regular cattle-market haunt for sex-seeking men and women – she had, suddenly and without warning, become almost embarrassingly drunk. Judy had, in Leila's words, 'sized-up' the sexual potency of the male contingent in almost universally scathing terms, and out of the whole nightclub only one man had remained unsavaged. Even Leila had been impressed with the survivor, and out of all Judy's friends, the twig was by far the most choosy – after all, she had men chasing her around left, right, and centre, and could afford to be.

Judy took a sip of her drink, unaware that the chief moron from the group at the bar was edging his way ever closer to her, his face flushed from swiftly-consumed alcohol and his smile uncomfortable from lack of practise.

According to Leila's sworn (Judy had made her) testimony, the man – the *God*, as Leila had insisted upon calling him – had approached her the instant she'd ventured through one of the nightclub's darker corners *en route* to the bar to buy another round of shots. A few words had been exchanged and then the man had moved his face close to hers and they had kissed. Then they had kissed again, more passionately, and then again, and things had quickly progressed from there.

By the time it was time to go home, Judy had been found sitting alone in a booth, a dopey look of satisfaction on her face, and the man was nowhere to be seen. But Leila had noticed right away that he'd left a calling card of sorts, in the form of a large dark love-bite on Judy's neck.

A vague, shadowy memory suddenly surfaced in Judy's mind now, of a pale-skinned face swimming very close to her face. She had felt his hot breath on her face as he spoke to her, but she couldn't tell what he was saying. It wasn't just the loud music that had prevented her from understanding him. The language he was speaking wasn't English. She had a feeling it wasn't any kind of language she'd ever heard before.

'Hello, darling, what's your name?'

Judy looked up, feeling suddenly hot and bothered. The first thing she saw was the waxy face of the God's Gift to Women Brigade, and the second was the sight of a very large, very strong male hand being placed on the moron's shoulder. He was pulled gently but firmly away from Judy, the expression of puzzlement that overtook his face quickly being replaced by one of brutish anger. He turned lumberingly around, his hands bunching into fists.

Then he stopped. His hands fell to his sides and his face, which Judy could now only see at three-quarters anyway, grew long and afraid. Judy twisted her head and saw the man who had intervened, and she instantly knew – though for the life of her she couldn't understand exactly *how* she knew – that this was the same man who had kissed her in the nightclub. The paler than pale complexion, the long jet black hair swept back imperially from a high, beautifully smooth forehead. He had a smell, too, she realised, a smell that cut through the scent of the rugby moron's toxic aftershave like a razor.

A sudden thrill of expectation ran through her as the moron faded unceremoniously into the background of her awareness and the stranger took centre stage. He turned and looked down at her, his hot eyes bizarrely chilling her with an animal but profoundly intelligent interest, and she found herself staring at his wide, full-lipped mouth as he turned yet again, this time to walk away.

Unconsciously, Judy silently rose to her feet and followed him leaving her unfinished drink, her handbag, and her coat behind without a second glance.

5

Fresh from her late night shower, Leila sat on her bed with her back pressed against the wall, clipping her toenails with an air of abstraction. It was ten to one in the morning and Tom had only left about forty minutes ago, after having waited for Judy to come home since around nine o'clock. He had left Judy's handbag and coat, which he had found abandoned in The Henry VII, in the girl's living room.

Initially, he had arrived at the flat full of anger – and also full of the story one of the bar-staff had told him, of Judy leaving the pub in the company of a man other than Tom. But by the time he'd gone back to his own bedsit all the anger had dissipated and he was as worried as could be.

It was the coat and handbag, of course, which had eventually got through to him. If Judy had taken off willingly with another man, why would she have left her things behind, especially her handbag, which contained her purse, credit cards, and the keys to her flat? He'd wanted to call the police when Judy wasn't home by midnight, to report her missing, and it had taken a major effort on Leila's part to stop him.

Eventually, as Tom's midnight deadline came and went, she'd managed to persuade him to wait, and told him that there would be a perfectly normal reason for Judy's absence. Perhaps it was normal for a guy as arrogant as Tom could be to believe that it would take something as dramatic as an actual abduction to make his girlfriend stand him up, that she would never do it by personal choice. But Leila knew that sometimes a new man could give off such a powerful chemical attraction for a woman that all reason and logic just flew out the window like a little bird. Something like that had happened to Leila herself in the past, more than once. It was like being under a spell.

So, Judy forgetting her coat and handbag in the pub? She could easily believe it, but it wasn't the kind of scenario she would be particularly comfortable explaining to any girl's boyfriend, and especially not Tom, especially with the mood he was in. It wasn't just the Judy situation that was bothering him, she could tell. Something else was disturbing him, although there was no way to know what it was. If he'd been her boyfriend, Leila could have got him to open up to her, but what the hell, he *wasn't* her boyfriend. That'd be Judy's problem when she came back.

If she came back.

Her small toenails now clipped, Leila spread herself out on the bed and stared up at the ceiling, wondering exactly what Judy was up to at this precise moment. Kissing the guy she'd met in the nightclub? Not if the way they'd been the other night was anything to go by, because if that was any kind of guide they'd be a long way past the kissing stage by now.

She imagined Judy enjoying the sensation of the guy's large hands slowly easing their way under the folds of the polo-neck sweater she'd chosen to wear, then lifting it, pulling it over her head, casting it aside. She imagined him bending his dark, feral head down over her arched neck, kissing all the way, to suck Judy's nipples into his wide mouth, nipping at them with his sharp white teeth.

Leila smiled to herself, absently popped the buttons on her pyjama jacket and slipped a hand under the stripy material to stroke her small breasts, teasing her nipples erect. Although she had no idea how Judy would have located her mystery man again, she couldn't really blame her for going for it. Sure, Tom could sometimes be nice, if he was in a good mood, but he was simply nowhere near as hot as the man in the nightclub. Leila shuddered a little as she remembered the smoothness of his pale complexion, the darkness of his eyes and the strong, almost cruel lines of his jaw and mouth.

Under her fingers, her tiny sharp nipples had swollen as her thoughts drifted away from any thought of Judy whatsoever, and centred in purely on the man. She closed her eyes as she felt a pleasant lubricity begin to coalesce between her legs, and her free hand snaked down over her chest and belly to find the pyjamas cord at her waist. After a moment's gentle tugging, the bow in the white cord unravelled and the trousers gaped open, exposing her tight, fuzzy box of pubic hair and the fork of her slim thighs opening wide. She ran her palm, now slightly sweaty, down over her belly and then pushed her fingers into the glistening hair below, and then further, slowly, deep into the succulent wetness of her−

'That looks like fun,' Judy's voice said into the silence of the room.

Leila's eyes snapped open and she sat up, swiftly pulling the gaping pyjamas until they covered most of her body again. She was blushing furiously with embarrassment at having being discovered masturbating, and she turned on Judy angrily.

'What the hell do you think you're−'

Leila's outburst caught in her throat the moment she really saw Judy, who seemed to have appeared out of nowhere to stand beside her bed. The neck of her polo neck sweater was hanging down over her shoulder and breast in fibrous tatters, as though it had been savaged by an aggressive animal, and there was dark, half-dried blood all over her mouth, jaw and neck.

But even this astonishing sight was superseded in strangeness by the man who stood beside her – the man from the nightclub.

His skin, so pale the other night, was now completely, almost blindingly white, and the mouth she had thought attractive in the dim shadows was even more badly blood-stained than Judy's. He seemed at this moment to be incredibly, almost unfeasibly tall, so much so that Leila found herself amazed that he was able to stand upright in the room. The whites of his dark eyes were suffused with blood, and, from his tear ducts, tiny crimson droplets had leaked out and run down his cheeks. The random patterns they had made almost looked deliberate, like primitive body art.

Leila suddenly glanced from the man to Judy and then back again, and realised that under the layers of blood their faces were almost the same now – cold and hard, and filled with an insatiable hunger.

Judy took a step toward the bed and Leila, terrified, leapt up to her feet intending to run, but found herself hampered by her loose pyjamas. She screamed when Judy caught her jacket as she made for the bedroom door, but she managed to wriggle and twist her way out of the material, only for the trousers to fall around her ankles, tripping her up.

Incredibly strong hands placed themselves beneath her arms and Leila was quickly pulled to her feet, where she stood supported by the two intruders. She wanted to struggle from their clutches, but the longer they held on to her, the weaker her resolve became. She looked fearfully away from the man's chalk-like face, his piercing eyes, and stared at Judy – or rather, at the creature she had become.

Despite her fear, Leila found her gaze drawn to the generous view of Judy's ample cleavage that the ripped sweater afforded her. And the more she looked at her flatmate's ripe body, and the more she thought of her earlier sexual fantasy about the man, the more she became aware that she was *enjoying* the feel of their hands on her body – especially now as they were not just holding and restraining her, but actually caressing her.

The man began to run his long tongue along the narrow slope of Leila's shoulder, and then closed his lips on the flesh of her neck to bestow a passionate love-bite. She could feel his teeth penetrating her skin and she grew faint with pleasure. Meanwhile, Judy had bent low to flick Leila's small nipples with her wet tongue, sending further sensual shock-waves through her body.

When Judy eventually sank her teeth into Leila's breast, the thin girl moaned in ecstasy, her head lolling back on her shoulders as she began to feel a delicious emptiness to her limbs that left her with a light-headed buzz of pleasure.

A little while later, Leila managed to find the strength to open her eyes. In her dressing room mirror, she could see streaks of blood flowing from wounds on her neck and breasts, while the creatures which fed from her appeared only as insubstantial phantoms, as crimson shadows cast against the growing paleness of her own body.

Leila closed her eyes once more.

The moment was too good to waste.

6

Tom closed the front door behind him, pocketing the bunch of keys Professor Palmer – in his typically illogical way – had chosen to send him in that morning's post. The note which had accompanied the keys in the Jiffy bag had told him that the house would be empty, and standing in the musty hallway now, Tom could well believe that it had been empty for years.

The whole place smelled uncared for, dirty and unaired, and Tom suddenly asked himself why he had taken Palmer up on this strange invitation – but was then able to supply the answer all too easily: curiosity. The stuff that croaked the cat.

His curiosity had even been strong enough to divert him from the search for Judy, which he'd intended to pursue first this in the morning. Instead of which, after receiving the package, all he'd had time to do was phone the girls' flat, from which there had been no answer. Even Leila seemed to have disappeared now, and he wondered if there could be some kind of connection. His mind kept trying to show him images of Judy with this other mysterious man, which only made him angry. Then they came back and showed him Leila there as well, a part of the deception, the final part of a bloody ménage a trois. He *knew* he should have questioned her more closely.

'Shut up,' Tom told himself angrily. 'Judy's all right. She's not in danger, and she's not up to anything behind your back. It's all a misunderstanding.' Saying it and hoping that it was true, and knowing, deep down, that it probably wasn't.

He shook his head to clear the worrying subject from his mind, and then he stepped forward and glanced up the long staircase.

'Hello?' he called to the house in general, for some reason hoping that Palmer would be home after all. 'Hello?'

There was no answer.

Tom walked though the first door to his left – as per his noted instructions – and found himself in what had to be Palmer's study, a large room lined with shelves of books on archaeology and ancient civilisations. On every other available surface were stacks of ancient tools, ornaments, and other artefacts, most of which had to be thousands of years old. Heavy lined curtains were drawn against the sharpness of the morning light, only a muted glow leaking through here and there, and a huge old desk dominated the centre of the room, covered in loose rolls of time-yellowed parchment. It was the sort of treasure-trove that Tom could see himself growing to love, completely losing track of time as he perused its mysteries.

Now, however, he simply didn't have the time.

In the corner of the room were the TV and old VCR the note had said would be there, with an equally old video camera set up on a tripod nearby. All Tom had to do now was turn everything on, press play on the VCR, and then sit back to find out what was going through the Professor's little mind this time. He found the single mains switch for the machines and flipped it on, then he set the VCR running and retired to the swivel chair behind Palmer's desk, where he made himself comfortable.

While Tom waited for the electronic snow-storm on the TV screen to be replaced by the images on the tape, he noticed that under one of the parchments on the desk was a large pile of what looked like wooden kebab skewers, except that they were made of a very old, very dark wood, which was possibly petrified.

The TV screen suddenly cut to black, and Tom sat back in the chair, absently fiddling with one of the skewers. A moment later the black was replaced onscreen by an image of the very desk at which he now sat.

There was a brief hiss of static as the camera's inbuilt microphone was switched on, and then Tom watched Palmer walk into shot and sit behind his desk. The two men now appeared to be studying each other from different pockets of time.

'Shit, Prof',' Tom whispered to himself. 'You look like absolute shit...'

He closed his mouth abruptly when Palmer cleared his throat and prepared to speak.

7

Leila's body was cold and stiff, and when she tried to move she was in agony. She opened her eyes, but found her inner darkness unrelieved even though her bodyclock told her that it had to be morning, and maybe as late as noon. However, even in the dead of night, some light managed to filter through her blinds – from the street lights, from the moon – and she couldn't imagine what was stopping it now.

She twisted herself over on to her side, discovering – through the silken whisper of flesh on flesh – that she was still naked, and in that moment she recalled in its entirety the attack she has sustained from Judy and...and *that* man. If he was a man at all, which she now doubted. Her trembling fingers settled uncertainly around the lamp at the side of her bed, and she grasped it fiercely, as though it were a lifeline.

Attack? Is that what it had been, really? Hadn't she encouraged them both, for the feel of their lips on her body and their hungry sucking – first tender and then passionate?

Leila groaned in the darkness and her voice was ragged, hoarse. She turned on the lamp and instantly curled away from the painful light, hiding her eyes. She lay there for a moment, recovering from the light's unexpected power, her eyes gradually opening, warily, to take in the strange condition of her room, and of herself.

Her naked body was stark white and it lay on the mattress with a horrid, dead weight, and Leila thought that she had never felt so heavy and lethargic in her whole life. There were streaks of dried blood over her breasts, stomach and thighs, but they were minimal, as though much greater quantities had been wiped off – or licked off. Of the bite wounds she knew she had suffered, there were no obvious signs. She could neither feel the wounds, nor sense their presence by touch.

It took an effort, and made Leila's head throb terribly, but she managed to sit up a little. On the floor beside the bed was the small striped heap of her pyjamas, and her shallow breathing came a little faster as she dwelt on the frightening and sensual manner of their removal. Then, in a raking sweep, her eyes leapt to the window, struggling to comprehend what possible purpose had been served by covering it with her duvet.

Why would Judy and the man do such a thing?

And how – she suddenly found herself thinking, peering sharply – had they managed to secure it in place by driving a series of thin wooden darts deep into the walls? How strong could the man be, and how strong had Judy grown in his company?

8

Palmer looked out of the TV screen and managed a weak, half-smile that made Tom's stomach turn over. It wasn't because the smile was so insincere that it was chilling. It was chilling because it had obviously been so difficult for the Professor to achieve.

Even at a distance from the screen, Tom was able to see the gaunt tiredness of Palmer's face, his bloodshot eyes. It was the face of a man who had been to hell and back, or believed that he had.

'Hello Tom, I'm very sorry to have brought you here like this,' Palmer said. 'In fact, I'm doubly sorry, because if you are viewing this tape, it means that I am dead. *Ipso facto*, this means that the task I have undertaken now passes on to you. I'll give you my reasons for choosing you a little later on, but first I think I'd better tell you everything – all the way from the beginning.'

'What the fuck are you on, Prof',' Tom whispered under his breath, but he continued to watch and listen intently.

Onscreen, Palmer reached down to his left and pulled a new bottle of tequila out of one of the desk drawers and uncapped it. 'A personal favourite,' he told Tom, 'but there's quite a selection down there – name your poison and help yourself. I think you're going to need a drink before you leave this house.'

While Palmer began to drink the tequila – without bothering with the niceties of a glass – Tom pulled open the drawer in question to find half-full bottles of gin, whisky, and vodka. He shook his head in disapproval and tuned back to the TV, where Palmer had lowered his bottle, gasping at the alcohol's bite.

'Now,' the Professor sighed, his eyes redder than ever, 'where were we?'

'At the beginning, you jerk,' Tom told him, exasperated as always at what he saw as Palmer's dithering.

'Ah yes, at the beginning...'

The Professor stared at the camera, and by proxy, at Tom, unsettling the student with the force of his conviction.

'I want you to promise me one thing, Tom. I know this isn't a lecture, I know it has nothing to do with your course, and I know that I have no authority over you in this matter... and I also know that it was wrong of me to treat you the way I have... but I'm asking you, *begging* you, even if you don't believe what I'm about to tell you, don't walk out on me. Wait until I've finished, please, and then try to accept that I know what I'm talking about. Open your mind to the truth...'

In the Professor's seat, Tom shrugged. 'Get on with it, you old windbag,' he said. 'I'll listen, but I'm promising nothing else.'

Palmer took another long swig from his bottle and then cleared his throat again.

'In the summer recess before you arrived at the university, I organised a field-trip to South America for myself and a few post-graduates who still had time on their hands and funds at their disposal. We had a local guide to show us around the points of interest. You know the sort of things – ancient burial sites, ruined ziggurats and ransacked tombs. Nothing ground-breaking, but still Indiana Jones enough to be relatively exciting for the younger people...

'One day, however, I wandered off from the main group and climbed into what I took to be a shallow cave, but closer examination proved it to be merely the mouth of a much deeper fissure, and, as it turned out, the beginning of an entire sequence of tunnels and cavern chambers...

'Now, I had read about the area extensively, and yet I had never heard of these caves, not even as rumours, and I was thoroughly intrigued at the possibilities for exploration and study they offered. We had brought some basic climbing gear along with us and so I decided to lead my small team into the cave as far as I thought it was safe to go. But when the time came to make our descent, our guide grew extremely agitated and told us that it wasn't safe in the caves, that there were ghosts and spirits in there. Naturally, we ignored his superstitions and carried on, taking plenty of provisions with us, and leaving him to wait at our camp outside the cave entrance to await our return…

'I will not speak now of the many natural wonders we saw down there by torch and lamplight. I will not elaborate of the geological beauty of that magical underworld, although it was considerable. That is not germane to the issue. What *is* important is that after spending four days exploring and wandering around the cave system, I stumbled upon a very special burial chamber, carved into the rock itself as if by the hand of a giant. The crude walls were covered in complex and ancient Aztec hieroglyphs, many of which even I was unfamiliar with, and in the centre of the chamber itself was a stone sarcophagus, covered with even more of the unknown symbols. Inside this sarcophagus, we found a mummy, completely undefiled, undisturbed for thousands of years. I do not need to tell you what this meant to me...'

While Palmer interrupted his tale for another belt of tequila, Tom found himself sitting on the edge of his seat, gripping the wooden skewer tightly in his hands, the palms of which had grown sweaty.

'Come on, come on,' he couldn't restrain himself from urging the video image. Palmer's standard lectures had never been as interesting as this. 'Get on with it, you old fart!'

9

Leila awoke from a feverish doze and awful, irrational dreams that were full of blood – blood, sex, and death – and when she sat up she was pleased to note that most of her aches and pains seemed to have vanished. In fact, despite all that had happened, she realised that she felt pretty good. Far, far healthier and stronger than she would ever have believed after losing so much blood.

The only unpleasant physical sensation remaining was a nagging hunger that seemed not to spread from her stomach but to encompass the whole of her body. She could not explain this odd feeling in any other way except to say that her body required sustenance on a massive scale.

Perhaps that was why she had awoken at this moment, or was it the influence of a powerful but strangely familiar smell which seemed to fill the air around her. It was a beautiful, richly attractive odour, but what was it? Somehow she felt that it was some kind of food.

The thin girl crawled off the bed and made her way over to the duvet-covered window, and then tried to pull the material aside to peek out. Immediately she snatched her hand away with a small hiss of pain – the duvet had been hot, hot, hot, as though it were holding back the cruel flames of an enormous fire, a destructive conflagration that would consume her if she once showed it her face.

The sun, she thought instinctively. The sun is bad for me now.

Leila turned away and sniffed the air again, wondering what the scent might be. She knew that it wasn't a food she knew well, but she knew it was *some* kind of food from the way her body was reacting to it. If her mind didn't know it, then her flesh did.

She followed her nose, sniffing her way about her bedroom until she came to the built-in wardrobe. All her senses told her that the thing she sought was inside, and she pulled the door open so savagely that it all but came off its hinges. Inside, half-hidden beneath a multi-layered curtain of clothes lay the bound and gagged body of a middle-aged man. He had been stripped of clothes and his whole body had been lacerated in thousands of places, wreathed in long scratches both deep and wide.

Palmer's eyes flickered open as the lamplight reached his face and then grew alarmingly wide as he focused on the young girl who crouched above him and stared down, completely unmindful of her nakedness. He saw a powerful shudder run through her slim body as she was overtaken by some sensory pleasure that seemed to rival sexual orgasm, and she leant over the length of his body, dropping to all fours, until her face almost came to rest upon his grey-haired chest. She was breathing deeply, rasping, and then, from the back of her throat, came a noise that sounded very much like a snarl. An animal snarl.

He became aware then of his own nakedness, as the girl first began to press her small firm breasts against him, pressing them into his lap, then brushing them back and forth over his beer belly as she started to lap at the small wounds on his chest and neck. As she did so, the bestial noises she made grew louder and louder. Palmer tried to scream around the gag in his mouth, but he found it impossible.

Leila, drooling now and luminous-eyed, suddenly stood up and dragged Palmer out of the closet like he was an old doll. Without any apparent effort, she lifted him entirely clear of the floor and then tossed him – almost casually – on to the bed. She followed him down quickly, laying herself out by his side like a lover.

She began to caress his wounded body with her small white hands aqua-gliding over the sea of perspiration that had sprung out of his pores, mixing with the dry but still intoxicating narcotic blood until it almost drove her insane with hunger. Now she knew for certain that she had died.

Died and been reborn.

After a while, Leila was satisfied that Palmer was fully aroused despite the terror she could see in his rolling, bloodshot eyes. She pushed herself up on to her knees and then straddled the older man's trembling body, gently taking his rigid penis, dark with pulsing blood, in her white, white hands and stroking it lightly, lovingly.

Leila smiled down at the man beneath her, feeling the sharp canine teeth emerging from beneath her lips as her hunger peaked. Then, teasing the very tip of Palmer's penis with a short fingernail, she walked a small distance backwards on her knees and dropped her head into his lap, resting her mouth on his penis and feeling him twitch in her fingers. He gave a small groan, and whether it was a groan of pleasure or fear she neither knew nor cared.

Grinning a small, wicked grin, she flicked out her tongue to torment Palmer just a little more. She had time. After all, just one swift bite down here when he was in this condition and the blood would pump out of him like water from a tap.

And in any case, Leila thought, nibbling and licking, ever since I was a child, I always enjoyed playing with my food.

10

Tom stared at the first faint streaks of dawn-light as they broke through the wooden roller-blinds which covered the windows of his bedsitter. His whole body felt sticky, and the sickly odour of sweat which came from beneath his duvet reminded him of just how badly his rest had been disturbed by Palmer's practical joke.

That bloody recording!

Even though he had rejected the Professor's stupid tale of ancient South American vampires and their resurrection in modern day England as pure nonsense, Tom had still been unable to get the subject off his mind. As a result, he'd been plagued by bad dreams all night long.

In a condition he now saw as a kind of delirium, he had dreamed of Palmer living through the fateful moments he had described for the camera, beginning with the long process of smuggling the mummy back into this country, and then the even longer process of deciphering the complex, unknown hieroglyphs and discovering the mummy's supposed nature.

'A vampire mummy, no less,' Tom thought now disgustedly, rubbing his tired and sleepy eyes. 'Talk about mixing the genres. Talk about pure Palmer bullshit.'

Nevertheless, drowning in a hot pool of his own perspiration as he slept, restless and uncomfortable, Tom had seen the ceremonial wrappings being slowly removed from the mummy's withered body. He had seen the wooden darts – presumably the same glorified kebab skewers as those on the desk – being removed one by one from its hard, blackened flesh. He'd seen Palmer, white-faced and almost fanatical, murmuring aloud the incantations he had copied from the tomb walls and sarcophagus and duplicated for just that moment.

'*Allegedly* copied,' Tom reminded himself, for although he had been interested despite himself – and yes, he had to admit to it, even excited – at the time he had watched the recording, it had only been a few short hours before he'd realised the idiocy of Palmer's claims. A dead body regenerating itself after two thousand years drying out in a cave. A mummified corpse coming back to life and escaping into the city night to drink its victims' blood. The man was cracking up, it was obvious. First the book on vampire lore he'd forced upon Tom, and now the ludicrous tape.

'What next?' Tom asked his bedsitter's ceiling.

What next indeed.

Tom frowned suddenly, growing wary now. Palmer was victimising him, and if this persecution was going to continue along the present lines, something would have to be done. It was no longer a question of different personalities clashing or a minor case of plagiarism on Tom's part – it was now a question of sanity, or the lack of it.

On the tape, Palmer had practically been in tears as he described his imagined actions. By the time he had informed Tom that he'd chosen him to be his protégé – in the event of his "untimely demise" –

because he respected Tom's strength of will and his intellect, the lecturer really was crying. Despite himself, Tom had to admit that Palmer had proved himself to be a very capable actor. Either that or he actually *believed* what he was saying, incredible as it all was. Tom could still hear his voice now...

'*...you're still young, Tom, you have an open mind...if you believe in nothing else, please believe this...if you don't, if you can't...by now you should have read the book of vampires I gave you, and as preposterous as it may seem, everything that you really need to know is in there...watch out for him at the locations I have already mentioned...do not let him see you...take the darts with you everywhere...you know what must be done...you must know that it has to be done...*'

'Fucking nutcase,' Tom muttered.

He reached out of the duvet and found the phone on the floor and pulled it up into bed with him. He dialled Judy's number, only to hear the now standard unbroken ringing. He swore loudly.

Well, that was it as far as Tom was concerned. The end. End of relationship, end of friendship, end of the temporary loans of money, goods, and services, end of dissertation editing and proofing favours, the end of *everything*. It was all over, there was no more. As soon as he could get hold of Judy, he'd tell her what he thought of her (he'd already worked out some beauties) and wish her the best of luck with her new life – as a complete and utter cheating bitch.

Tom laid the phone back on the floor, half hanging out of his bed in the process, and remained there as he found his antagonistic thoughts being disturbed by gentler emotions. The end, he thought again, a little less gleefully than before. The end of intimacy, sexual and otherwise, the end of affection. The end of so many joyful and ultimately self-deluding post-coital dreams, fantasies that they had shared...love...a home...kids...

At that precise moment, Tom stopped thinking about Judy and their ruined relationship. He stopped thinking any rational thoughts whatsoever. He simply stared in pop-eyed horror at the hand which lay on the threadbare carpet at the foot of his bed. Slowly, like a man in a dream (or a man who wished her were in a dream), he sat up and crawled down the length of his bed. On the way he caught a sight of himself in the wall mirror, and saw that his face resembled that of a man trying to swallow an extremely bad medicine.

Tom peered over the end of his bed and his heart convulsively bounded about in his chest, a mad jumping-jack with little idea of its limitations or restraints.

On the floor lay Professor Palmer's naked corpse.

There was no question that he could be alive. His skin had been randomly torn from head to toe, and in his dead eyes was the expression of madness which comes to those who have seen the true way of things, the truth that extends beyond truth and becomes ugly myth and cruel legend made real.

It took a long time for Tom's eyes to traverse the monument to atrocity that was Palmer's abused body, and not one detail was lost to his startled gaze. The small folds of yellowing flesh, pulling away from the hundreds of scratches and tears like melting plastic;

the deep but completely anaemic scars left by the cords he had once been bound by; and the gag, jammed savagely into his mouth, foul with vomit and mucus.

The final thing he saw – as though sweet, comic fate had saved this sumptuous delicacy for the very last treat – was the total absence of genitalia.

At first Tom tried to tell himself that the poor man had only been castrated with a knife. Then he looked a little closer, his curiosity morbid as a hungry vulture's, and he saw the ragged ends to the wounds – the rough-edged tears and the...the teethmarks.

'Teethmarks?' he asked himself in shock. 'Teethmarks?'

Without allowing another moment to pass, Tom bent swiftly forward, gagging, his stomach contracting violently, and he vomited directly into Palmer's dead face.

It just wasn't the Professor's day.

11

Tom sat behind Palmer's desk again, and this time he took advantage of the Professor's alcohol. He raised his chosen bottle in salute to the TV screen as he replayed Palmer's tape for the fourth time in succession, and then quickly poured a huge amount of whisky down his throat. In his other hand, Tom held one of the wooden darts, and as the alcohol began to burn its merry way through his system he found himself gripping it tightly enough for its tip to almost break his skin.

It was ten o'clock in the evening. Too late in the day to do anything more practical than sit here drinking, and to Tom's weary and befuddled mind it seemed much later. The whole day had flown past him as he'd attempted to cope with the shock of discovering Palmer's corpse in his room. Not an easy task, considering that he also had to get his head around the fact that the Professor's story was actually true, and also that – and this was genuinely terrifying – the vampire must have been *in* his bedsitter while he was asleep and left the body as a warning to any would be vampire-killers in the vicinity.

Namely, himself.

'Fucking awesome,' Tom said, his voice now slurred a little by his alcohol intake. This was a phrase he had been using with increasing frequency as the day passed and which had made its first appearance as he'd wrapped Palmer's body in one of his bed-sheets, trying hard not to look too closely at, or indeed to touch, the bloodless, rubbery-looking flesh. The same phrase – if he remembered correctly – had also been used to great effect later, when, under cover of darkness, he transported the corpse back to Palmer's house in an old Ford Fiat he'd borrowed from a friend.

Now Palmer's body was safely and discreetly tucked away in the house's downstairs lavatory, and, as he sat at the desk watching the tape over and over, drinking the Professor's whisky, and trying to think up an immediate plan of action, Tom reflected that if he never again said anything different in his entire lifetime, that phrase alone could make up for the loss. It was, undoubtedly, the best – in fact, the only – phrase suited for the job in hand.

The situation was fucking awesome.

Tom glanced back at the TV screen just as Palmer concluded his account of the vampire' activities and warned him, yet again, to be extremely cautious in his approach to their 'little problem', as the Professor insisted on referring to the unnatural creature he had brought back into the world. Tom scowled angrily at the image of Palmer's haggard face.

'What the hell have you got me into, you meddling old fool?' he asked bitterly as Palmer abruptly vanished from the screen, replaced by a hissing field of electronic fuzz and static.

Apathetically, Tom allowed the recording to run, realising that there was no more to be gained from rewinding and watching it again. He took another drink instead, and when that tasted good to him, he took another. He was considering the low level left in the bottle and wondering what else Palmer had in his little drinks cabinet when he looked up at the TV sharply. The fuzz was being replaced by a series of converging horizontal lines, inbetween which Tom could see fresh images. The tape had obviously been used more than once.

Tom stared at this new development with bleary interest and was quickly rewarded as the picture resolved itself – only to reveal exactly the same shot of Palmer sitting behind his desk with the same scrolls and darts in front of him.

Everything was the same, except that Palmer himself looked healthy. Clean-shaven and refreshed, he was pointing to one of the open scrolls with a self-satisfied smile on his face, and Tom came to the conclusion that this was a recording the Professor must have made prior to the vampire's resurrection and accidentally taped over in his later confusion.

As this thought crossed Tom's mind, the video's sound finally kicked in and he could hear Palmer saying something about the unusual story told in the parchments and his intention to carry out the strange ceremony detailed there. A ceremony which included the reading of the Aztec incantations and a liberal amount of blood – which Palmer claimed he would 'borrow' from the University's medical research department.

The Professor then passed on from the scrolls to speak about the wooden darts he'd pulled – just that morning – from the vampire's mummified remains. He gently held one of the darts up for the camera's inspection as he spoke:

'You will observe,' the dead man's image said, 'that these darts have a marked similarity to those still used today by many South American tribes as ammunition for their blowpipes – usually tipped with the lethal poison *curare*...'

At this point, Tom's heart skipped a beat and his hand opened in a violent reflex action, allowing the dart he had been holding so firmly to fall to the floor. He stared at his fingers and palm with a kind of blank hysteria, looking with fearful paranoia for a tiny trickle of blood leaking from a fresh wound...and there it was! He had actually managed to puncture the thick flesh at the base of his thumb, and as he realised the implications of this injury a low, painful moan escaped his throat and the whisky bottle slipped from his suddenly nerveless fingers. The bottle landed with a dull thud and its remaining contents began to wash out over the carpet.

'However,' Palmer continued, his tone dismissive, 'in this case the darts are so ancient that my forensic tests have shown there to be no evidence of any existing poison, *curare* or otherwise...'

In a riot of indignation, Tom shot to his feet and literally screamed at the TV screen. The relief he felt was enormous, but compared to the fear Palmer had just subjected him to, it was nothing.

'You stupid, stupid bastard!' he shouted at the Professor's image.

All his anger was directed at the man who had made the recording – and not the man who had recently died under horrific circumstances. At this moment, Tom just had to give vent to that anger or explode.

'You frightened the life out of me!' he yelled. 'You stupid old bastard, what the hell did you think you were doing?'

Furious, Tom used the remote control to turn the TV off. In the sudden silence that followed he fell back into the chair and unaccountably found himself crying into his hands. The contrasting emotions of the day had finally caught up with him and he gave himself up to their tearful consequence with the same lack of restraint as he had his anger. This petulant bout of crying quickly turned into a sobbing fit which drew its strength from his troubles in the past day.

'I'm bloody well entitled to this,' he said to himself, belligerent despite his tears. 'In the last twenty-four hours I've lost my girlfriend to a stranger, found a dead man at the bottom of my bed, and discovered there's a real, undead and kicking vampire out there who's probably got me on his personal menu...'

12

Tom woke up slowly, feeling heavy and unrefreshed, knowing that the alcohol that had helped him fall asleep would also have left him with a stinking headache. He opened his eyes to the gloom of Palmer's study – only broken by the TV's fizzing screen – and realised that it was still night-time, and that he must have slept for no more than twenty or thirty minutes. He sat up from his slumped and awkward position in the chair and hissed as a sharp pain shot through his shoulder and neck. He began to massage his aching limbs, but then abruptly stopped.

In the doorway, smiling across at him, stood Professor Palmer. He was still naked and seemed blissfully unaware of both the scars that covered every inch of his skin and the bloodless hole where his penis used to be. With a friendly nod of acknowledgement, Palmer winked at Tom and then lifted a hand to his mouth and began examining his teeth with his fingers. His smile – which seemed to be perpetual – grew wider still as he located his elongated canines.

Under his breath, Tom whispered, 'Fucking awesome...'

As if on cue, another figure, small and wiry, walked into the room, pushing past the fledgling vampire without a care. It only took a moment to realise that it was Leila and then he was on his feet, a bunch of wooden darts clamped in his hand like a knife.

'Get over here, Leila! Stay away from him, that isn't Palmer anymore!' He gestured for the girl to join him behind the desk, and as she did so he put his arm protectively around her narrow shoulders. 'What are you doing here?'

'I came here looking for Judy. Somebody told me they'd seen her with Professor Palmer.' Leila was pursing her lips together so that she wouldn't burst into laughter. 'What's wrong, Tom? What's going on?'

'That's not the Professor,' Tom told her, a tremor in his voice. 'It used to be, but he's a vampire now.'

Keeping a close eye on Palmer, who seemed content for the moment to watch their exchange with benign interest, he glanced swiftly around the shadow-filled room, trying to see if there was a crucifix somewhere, or a copy of the bible among the shelves of books. Anything. His efforts were in vain, and he looked down at Leila, more afraid for her than he was for himself.

'I know it sounds crazy, but I'm telling the truth. Vampires exist.'

Leila could no longer restrain herself and she grinned widely, nudging Tom in the ribs. 'I know *that*, stupid! What's your problem?'

Tom stared at her, shocked. 'What the hell are you...' The words dried up in his mouth when he caught a glimpse of the sharp canines now protruding over her bottom lip, and as realisation hit him he slumped back into the chair. 'You... you're one, too.'

'That's right,' Leila cheerfully replied. 'So is Judy. She'll be along later, so you can see for yourself.' She gleefully watched as horror transformed Tom's face into a delightfully comical mask. 'Don't get so worked up about it all,' she advised him with a giggle. 'It isn't so bad. It's sort of nice.'

'Hey, Tom?' Palmer called from the doorway, his awful toothy smile now rueful and – Tom thought – almost fatherly. 'You want to watch out for that one,' he said, nodding at Leila. 'She'll bite your bollocks off if you're not careful.'

Tom's eyes once again dropped to the empty space between Palmer's legs and he gaped. 'Sweet Jesus, you don't mean...?'

'Yeah, sorry about that, Prof',' Leila said with very little regret in her voice.

Palmer only shrugged. 'That's life.'

'You see,' Leila said, sitting down on Tom's lap, 'what you have to understand is that when I got to the Prof' here I was famished, absolutely *famished*.' She plucked the bunch of darts from Tom's grip and tossed them on the desk. 'Furthermore, it was my first real taste of blood, and I'm afraid I got a little bit carried away. It's my favourite piece of the male anatomy anyway, but once the blood started flowing... Wow!'

Palmer nodded at Tom sagely. 'Pretty orgasmic, I must admit.'

'But let me reassure you,' Leila continued, 'I've had a bit more practise since then and I've got it all under control – you'll have nothing to worry about and everything to enjoy.'

'Now wait a minute,' Tom said, perspiring heavily now and trying to wiggle out from underneath the little girl, who had suddenly seemed to have dramatically increased in weight and density. 'You're not going to take me, I'm not going to end up like Palmer, I don't want to—'

'Now sit still, Tom!' Leila said sharply, giving him a hard, mesmeric stare until he did just that. 'Don't be such a baby. Everyone's nervous at first, but they soon get over it. You'll see.'

Leila slipped out of his lap, suddenly as boneless as a snake, dropped to her knees and spread his legs. She began to run her hands up and down his inner thighs, teasing him until she saw a bulge appear in his trousers. 'It'll be fun when you're one of us,' she said, reaching out to unbuckle his belt. 'We're all going out together tomorrow night. Judy's arranged something special for us at the nurses' home near the hospital...and you *know* what they say about nurses...'

'Judy!' Tom managed to gasp.

'Don't you worry about Judy,' Leila said, pulling down his zip. 'She won't mind you being unfaithful now. In fact, to tell you the truth, she's quite hung up on that Mexican guy, although he's a little too macho for my taste.'

'I think you'll find that he's an Aztec, actually,' Palmer butted in smugly.

Leila turned her head to glare at Palmer, who was leaning forward and watching her actions keenly, hungrily. 'Excuse me, Professor,' she said, impatiently. 'Any chance you could give us a little privacy here?'

41

Palmer held up his hands in apology. 'Sorry, sorry. Didn't mean to intrude. I think I'll pop out for someone to eat.'

'Good idea,' Leila approved. 'And you'd better put some clothes on, for God's sake. You're hardly a pin-up now, you know.'

With a nod and a final smile, Palmer excused himself and headed off into the night while Leila turned all her attention back to Tom. She reached out and grabbed the waistband of his jeans and then dragged them and his underwear down to his knees at the same time.

'I don't...' Tom croaked. 'I don't...'

'Of course you do,' Leila said softly and persuasively as she took him firmly in hand. 'And so does this little chap down here...'

Tom tried to drag himself out of the hypnotic trance Leila appeared to have put him in. He knew that he had to break free now, before it was all too late, before she had him completely within her power.

Out of the corner of his eye he saw the wooden darts scattered across the desk where Leila had tossed them, and he wondered if he could gather his remaining strength for one last effort and drive one into her heart. He took a deep breath and really thought he might be able to – and then he felt the tip of his penis slip between Leila's cold lips, her tongue caressing him with a cat-like rasp, and then he knew for certain that it was too late. He was lost.

With an electric thrill, Tom felt the twin sharpness of Leila's canines drag along the length of him, and without another thought he abandoned himself completely to the tumultuous ocean of dark pleasure in which he was drowning. So utterly entranced was he by Leila's attentions, that when she lifted her head for a moment, he groaned in dismay and actually urged her to continue.

'I will, I will,' Leila told him, 'don't worry about that. I only wanted to know what you said just then?'

'Said?' Tom shook his head blankly. 'What do you mean?'

'Oh well, it doesn't matter – you can tell me later, after I've finished.'

Tom wasn't aware that he had said anything at all, but, as Leila lowered her lovely head once more and the blood and the human life began to flow out of him, he reflected that it may well have been the whispered words:

'Fucking awesome...'

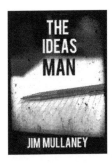

It can be hard to bear when you feel that you've been left behind in the great game of life — particularly if you also believe that you've been cheated into the bargain, as one of the characters in this story does. There's a longer, more crime-like version of this story somewhere in the depths of the vaults, too, but this is the original — short, and not-so sweet.

Terrance Milne carefully leaned back in his seat, watching the twinkling surface of the whisky in his refilled glass sway as he tried to settle himself against the cheap and nasty cushions that were threatening to crowd him out of the armchair. He took a small sip of the alcohol — also pretty cheap and nasty, in his estimation — and looked aimlessly around the pokey living room, attempting to close his ears.

Impossible to do, of course.

Even though the door to the equally pokey kitchen/diner was firmly closed, he could still hear the raised voices of Greg Bennett and his lovely wife Debbie as they exchanged a long series of hard words. Harsh words. Bitter, ugly words.

Milne raised his eyebrows and inhaled through his nose, thinking, *oh dear*. Thinking, *tut-tut. Well, well...*

Thinking that he knew his visit was the cause of the argument. Or maybe not his visit, exactly. Maybe it was just him.

Looking around the small living room was no real escape, either, being visually just about as loud as the argument next door, the furnishings and decor an injudicious mixture of overpriced tat and faux luxury materials. Faux leather, faux suede, faux animal print, faux art.

The smoked-glass coffee table ached to be retro but missed by a mile, and the bizarre three-piece suite that crowded the room like cars parked bumper-to-bumper was as unpleasant to the touch as it was to the eye, making Milne's palms itch whenever he touched it, as though it had been upholstered in rolls of fibreglass insulation. Black and white fronds of stylised bamboo in bas relief climbed the textured wallpaper and disappeared under the grainy polystyrene coving, presumably trying to get as far away from the carpet as was possible.

This was the kind of living room you always seemed to find in the background when people posted their home-made porn on the Internet, Milne thought to himself... with all the pot-bellies and cracked heels in the foreground, naturally.

Faux erotica.

Some of the smaller details on show were quite amusing, once you noticed them in amongst the texture/pattern overkill, and seemed to Milne's eye to reflect perfectly the entirely separate natures of the couple who lived here. Debbie Bennett's contribution to this domestic freak show was a selection of glass clowns, pixies sitting cross-legged on toadstools, and other similarly depressing rainy-day trophies from a succession of miserable seaside gift shops – all displayed without a single trace of kitsch self-awareness, naturally.

Against his will, but actually completely in line with his expectations of this nostalgic little trip down memory lane, Milne was rapidly coming to the conclusion that the Bennetts were no longer his type of people. Of course, Debbie never really *had* been his type, which was why he'd never taken advantage all those years ago when she'd really been throwing herself at him, offering him the key to the whole candystore.

Greg Bennett's contribution to the family nest was a determinedly single-minded collection of movie trivia. Framed prints of lurid posters were hung on the walls, accompanied by framed publicity stills, some of them signed by has-been actors, and stacks of reference books crowded on every shelf. They all had one predominant theme - the horror film.

No surprise there.

Greg Bennett and Terrence Milne had been close friends since the age of eleven, ever since they'd met at junior school and discovered they shared an avid, thoroughly pre-adolescent taste for the excesses of the horror film. Together they had delighted in every toothy vampiric kiss, giggled their way through every nude ritual sacrifice, and picked apart the stitches in every half-baked creation from Herr Doctor's laboratory.

Hammer Films, Amicus Films, Tyburn Films, and American International, as well as the old Universal classics, and a dozen others beside – all seen for the first time on late night TV. They had been an absolute obsession for the boys, but it seemed that Bennett was obsessed with them still, and their modern counterparts, as he approached forty years of age.

Milne looked from an image of Christopher Lee as the Count to one of old bacon-faced Freddy brandishing his razor-mitt, and then on to one of the deformed family from a modern series of gruesome shockers that had almost reached double figures in terms of sequels. He took another sip of his drink and shook his head sadly. It wasn't that he no longer cared for the subject – in fact, he was devoted to it – it was just that he was past such an obvious glorification as this.

His ego wouldn't allow it.

Milne no longer considered himself a fan. He had left the ranks of the watchers and had become instead one of the doers, but it had been a long journey that had taken the best part of two decades to achieve.

He'd left home as soon as he was able and worked his way through film school, and then struggled for a long time picking up bits and pieces of freelance work here, there and everywhere, before finally finding his niche directing TV commercials and pop promos. Eventually his reputation had grown sufficiently for him to raise enough finance for a short personal project that had played the European festival circuit with some success, winning a few awards and getting his name out there.

A couple of years later, his first feature film, a low-budget British-based chiller, had made his reputation critically, and his second, backed with

American money and set in the States, was now cleaning up at the US box office in a big way.

Bennett on the other hand, lacking his friend's over-riding motivation, drive, and ambition, had discovered another passion early in life and had subsequently married her, against Milne's advice and, quite obviously, to his own later regret. He'd drifted a long way from his daydreams of creative fame and fortune and had finally ended up as the warehouse manager of a small printing firm only a few miles from the school where the pair had first met as young boys.

It wasn't too bad there, Bennett had told him earlier during his visit, and he was almost happy.

He was *almost* happy, but not quite

The thing was, Milne knew that Bennett really wanted to be what his friend had become, but without all the hard work, sacrifices and terrible periods of uncertainty that had gone into achieving it. And Bennett *knew* that Milne had seen this envy in him, but both men had been at great pains to mutually ignore it this evening.

So far.

Bennett re-entered the room rather sheepishly and closed the door behind him. He wandered over to the settee trying to look calm, sitting down deliberately heavily in an attempt to elicit a little chuckle from Milne to cover his own embarrassment. It didn't work, so he shrugged and said, 'Women!' in what he hoped would be seen as a rueful, affectionate manner.

Again Milne didn't respond, although it was on the tip of his tongue to suggest to his friend that if he was so unhappy with his lot then there were ways out of such situations. Divorce. Separation. In the end he thought it was probably wiser to say nothing, which was to be his last half-sober decision of the night.

There was ten seconds of silence, and then Bennett broke the ice.

'Did you see *The Premonition*?' he asked enthusiastically, his voice too loud, even to his own ears. However, by sheer volume he managed to make it perfectly clear that he didn't want to talk about his marital problems.

'Yes, I did,' Milne replied, a note of deep reserve in his voice. 'Some of it, anyway. I walked out of the screening as discreetly as I could about halfway through. I personally found it very unimaginative.'

'The screening?' Bennett asked, surprised.

'I was invited by the director to see a rough-cut about eight or nine months ago,' Milne explained complacently. 'His producer and mine are big buddies, it turns out. They were both executives at Fox years ago.'

'Walked out of a director's screening?' Bennett smiled wryly. 'Good for you. I saw it on Netflix. I couldn't bring myself to walk out of my own home.'

'Sure,' Milne replied flatly, as though he wasn't quite convinced and didn't much care. 'But then you liked it, and I didn't.'

Bennett thought for a moment, trying to remember what else he had seen and enjoyed. Milne shook his freshly empty glass and was waved toward the bottle. He collected it and filled Bennett's glass before his own, spilling just a little on the coffee table, and then went back to his seat, finally giving up and throwing aside the cushion that only had the effect of making the chair even more uncomfortable than it really was.

Milne looked up to see Bennett pointing at him, struggling to find words, his face aglow and his eyes wide.

'*House of Evils*!' he said finally, triumphantly. 'What about that?'

Milne nodded his head wearily.

'I suppose it's not a bad example of its type,' he conceded without pleasure. 'Trouble is, its type has pretty much had its day, or should have by now. It's old school, sure, but not old school *good*. Let's face it, it's the same old routine we've seen a million times before. They get an actress to take most of her clothes off, cover her in fake blood, and then chase her through an old house with a Steadicam. How many times can you watch that shit? No, I'm sorry,' he ended firmly, 'but it's just not good enough anymore.'

This time Bennett was visibly irritated by his friend's superior manner. 'All right,' he said, the joy gone from his voice and face. 'How about *Skinnerman*?'

Milne all but curled up his lip at the mention of this particularly gory film.

'Absolute crap from beginning to end, man!' he said with immense conviction, waving a dismissive hand, as though trying to disperse a bad smell. 'Fucking straight-to-DVD torture-porn dogshit!'

'But the effects!' Bennett responded. 'There's no way you can accuse it of not having a good budget.'

'Look, I'm not talking about simple production value here,' Milne said as though explaining himself to a child. 'The effects are very impressive, of course they are, but where's the script? Where's the acting? Where's the story arc? Characters you care about? The direction is *terrible* and it looked as though it had been edited by an ox. The bald truth is that the CGI effects are vastly overused to hide the fact that the whole film isn't worthwhile. As I said at the start – absolute shit.'

'Jesus Christ!' Bennett exploded, throwing himself back in his seat. He nodded his head sharply, his lips tightly pressed together. His eyes were angry. 'It's all right for you,' he continued bitterly. 'With your designer clothes and your fancy car, and your actress girlfriend and your bloody name up on the screen. You can afford to nit-pick, you can afford to be blasé about these films, but I'm....'

Bennett stopped abruptly in mid-sentence, suddenly realising what a supreme fool he was making of himself. The two men looked each other in the eye and Bennett knew he'd managed to raise a barrier between them that he might never be able to remove. In the past he'd always tried to skirt around the subject of envy with Milne by pretending to be a devoted married man and a gourmet of the horror film. It was now plainly obvious that this tactic would not be open to him in the future, and he was mentally kicking himself for making his jealousy so obvious.

How best to back down, he wondered?

Milne swallowed more whisky and then studied his glass, turning it this way and that, fuzzily wondering how come it was almost empty again.

I shouldn't have come, he thought. I really shouldn't have come.

He looked up as Bennett cleared his throat.

Gazing down into his lap with a lop-sided smile on his face, Bennett chuckled and shrugged his shoulders. 'Sorry about that, Terry. A fight with Debs always puts me in a really foul mood. Please, forgive me.'

He looked up to meet Milne's hooded eyes. They were calm eyes. Amused eyes. He looked away again.

'Forget it,' Milne told him softly.

'I will, if you don't mind.' Bennett picked up his glass and raised it to Milne. 'Look, here's to the success of your new film,' he toasted.

Milne raised his own glass and said archly, 'Well, here's to the *continued* success of my new film...'

'Yes,' Bennett said. 'I read somewhere that it made ten million dollars in its first weekend.'

Milne laughed. 'Well, I don't know where you read that but it's not totally accurate. It made about nine million on the *Friday* – and that's just the domestic North American box-office, of course. Over the entire opening weekend, it did just over forty-two, which for an R-rated movie is pretty damn good.'

'Jesus. That's terrific.'

Bennett ran his eyes over Milne's extremely expensive casual clothes, remembering the Jag that was currently sitting on his short driveway instead of his own five-year-old Nissan, which was parked on the road. He remembered the extremely expensive leather travelling bag he'd put into the spare room earlier, and also the name of the extremely expensive hotel in London where Milne's beautiful Yank actress girlfriend was slogging her way through the press junket for the European release of her own new movie.

Earlier, over Debbie's bland home-cooked dinner, Milne had gone on and on about his new lifestyle. The rented house in Coldwater Canyon with its own pool. The stylists, the dieticians, the personal trainers, the feng shui advisors...and on and on. This was probably what had set Debs off in the first place.

'That's terrific,' he said again, in a smaller voice.

Milne had thrown the last of his drink down his throat and sloshed out another glassful. 'I'll send you and Debs a couple of tickets to the London premiere next month. Leicester Square, red carpet, the whole shebang. Should be a good night.'

'Thanks,' Bennett said. 'Appreciate it. Debbie won't be interested, but send two anyway... I might bring someone else.'

For the first time the ghost of an honest smile settled on Milne's lips. 'Have you got something going?' he asked.

'Maybe,' Bennett admitted. He looked down into his lap again as he struggled to remain silent, but the urge to confess was very suddenly very strong with him. 'You were right all those years ago,' he said. 'She *has* held me back. We're *not* suited.'

Now that he'd had the satisfaction of hearing it from Bennett's own lips, Milne was inclined to be generous.

'Oh, I don't know, Greg,' he said. 'How old was I when I said that stuff, and what did I know about *anything* then, let alone mature relationships? There must be something good between you. I mean, what is it now - fourteen, fifteen years down the road? That's a bloody long time to be with someone.'

'Yes, it is. But now all the love's gone. It went out the window with all the lost opportunities.'

'I'm so sorry,' Milne said gravely.

Well, well, well, he thought. Can I read people or can I read people? The poor son of a bitch.

Bennett sighed. 'Ah, what the hell. It's only life.'

In a pig's eye you're sorry, he thought. It's just another victory for you. Another success. Why are you always winning, Milne?

Because he steals, an angry, jealous little voice answered. *He steals*.

Bennett took another drink and felt the whisky burn a path through the last of his feeble stock of reserve.

'I was reading an article in some online magazine about your new film,' he said, his voice calmer than his temper. 'It was full of spoiler alert warnings, but I couldn't resist reading it. The article mentioned you had a particular scene in which a dismembered body is found hidden in a chest of drawers. Arms in one drawer, legs in another, and so on... Is that true?'

Milne nodded with a drunken smirk. 'It is.'

Bennett paused for a moment before speaking on what at first seemed like a different subject, biding his time.

'Hey, do you remember when we used to spend a lot of time down at the bowling alley in town?'

Milne laughed. 'Yes, I do. Only seems like yesterday, doesn't it? Hard to believe that it was over fifteen years ago.'

'Do you remember how we used to get too tanked up to bowl straight and then spend the rest of the night making up plots for horror films? Do you remember the evening we couldn't get a lane at all and spent the entire night in the bar?'

Milne let his blurry eyes drift up to the ceiling as he tried to recall this specific occasion. 'Yes!' he said suddenly. 'Yes, we were drinking pints as if they were going out of fashion! Man, I can't remember the last time I got that drunk.'

Unless it's now, Bennett thought.

'That night in the bar,' Bennett said quietly, 'that was when *I* thought up the idea of the body parts in the chest of drawers.'

Milne stared at him.

'Did you?' He looked thoughtful for a moment and then shook his head in wonder. 'That's amazing. Absolutely incredible memory you've got, and after all those beers.'

He took a large mouthful from his glass and smiled broadly, the alcohol increasing his appreciation of the questions he supposed were pure nostalgia.

'Those were good days, my friend,' he said. 'Very good days indeed.'

Bennett exhaled noisily, frustrated that Milne hadn't understood what he'd been getting at. He brooded for a while in silence, shaking his head from side to side when offered another drink, watching Milne pour yet another for himself even before the last was finished. He was on the way to getting very, very drunk.

Bennett cleared his throat.

'You know that scene in your first film where the man finally realises that his girlfriend isn't quite what she seems anymore? That the house has done something to her? Then he goes across to a decanter and pours himself a drink, but when he drinks it he finds that it isn't booze, it's blood.'

'That's right,' Milne cried gleefully. 'Man, the day we shot that scene was hilarious. What's-his-face, the actor, thought that we were using tomato juice to double for the blood, but while he was in make-up one of the props guys filled the decanter with some *real* blood, pigs' blood, he'd got from an abattoir.'

Milne was almost crying with laughter.

'What you see on the screen is a real reaction, not acting. He really did throw up after taking a mouthful!'

Bennett nodded without humour.

'Do you remember the weekend a few months before my marriage, when we went to Eastbourne? We stayed in that horrid little blue and white caravan by a stream, and it didn't have a toilet.'

Milne squinted in concentration. 'Had to piss in the stream, didn't we?'

'That's correct, and we spent the whole weekend making up plots for films.'

'Yes, and we drank a lot.' Milne's eyes were closed as he smiled to himself, alcohol happy. 'Good days indeed.'

Bennett gave himself a beat and then said, 'That's when I had the idea of the wine turning into blood, amongst others.'

Milne opened his eyes and stared at Bennett. He blinked a few times, his vision a hazy and unreliable. Far too much whisky in his system.

'What?' he asked.

'I said, that was the weekend when *I* made up something else that later appeared in one of *your* films.'

Milne sat back in his chair, passing a hand over his face. 'What are you trying to say?' he asked.

'You know damn well what I'm saying!' Bennett said angrily. 'You took my ideas and used them!'

Milne stood up uncertainly. 'Greg,' he said, 'I don't know what the hell you're insinuating, but–'

'I'm not *insinuating* anything.' Bennett stood up quickly, his balance much more certain, and took a few angry steps toward Milne. 'I'm saying you stole my ideas and got rich off them!' he shouted. 'You're a thief! A fucking thief!'

Milne's face dropped at the accusation.

'Don't be an idiot, Greg. I didn't *steal* your ideas, I can't even remember you telling me them! Besides, the things you've mentioned were just details, small details. I'm not sure they even came from me. I mean, wine into blood? That's in the fucking Bible, isn't it? Transubstantiation, or something. Did you make up the Bible, too?'

'No, but I–'

'And anyway, there are whole rafts of writers working on these films at any one time, most of them not even credited, and any one of them could have come up with that. You've got to remember that in the context of a whole film one small idea is nothing. Nothing at all. Grow up for Christ's sake!'

'I'm *not* an idiot.' Bennett took another step forward and held an outraged, pointing finger only an inch from Milne's face. 'And don't tell me to grow up!' he shouted at the top of his voice. 'You can't lie your way out of this. Who do you think you are?'

He placed a hand on Milne's chest and shoved him back into the armchair.

'Just who the *fuck* do you think you are?'

Suddenly the men heard a sharp series of knocks on the ceiling above their heads.

'Shut up!' they heard Debbie call down. 'For God's sake, I'm trying to sleep!'

Bennett whirled away and snatched a couple of the glass clowns from a shelf and threw one at the ceiling where it shattered and showered back down in a thousand glittering pieces. *'You* fucking shut up!' he screamed at the ceiling, throwing the second clown after the first. 'Who asked *you* to open your mouth, you fucking bitch!'

Bennett stood in the centre of the room, glaring at the ceiling with his fists clenched. His lips twitched convulsively but no words came from them. Milne stood staring in disbelief. He was swaying from side to side, much the worse for drink, and the violence of the situation had upset his stomach, making him feel like puking. The head of one of the broken clowns lay between his feet, having missed him by inches during its descent.

Milne looked at Bennett warily. He was cooling down, his breathing becoming slower, more controlled. He looked down from the ceiling and across at Milne. Some of the fire had gone out of his eyes, but not a great deal.

'I think I'd better find a hotel,' Milne said, slurring the words slightly. He leant forward in the armchair, steadying himself to stand up again.

Bennett took a deep breath. He wanted Milne to go, and he didn't care whether he ever saw him again, but he could see that the man was drunk. He wrestled with his conscience. 'You're not in a fit state to drive,' he said at length.

'I'll get a taxi.'

Bennett shook his head, struggling with his conscience. 'No,' he said grudgingly. 'You'll never get a taxi around here at this time. You'd better stay here, as we arranged. Just because we've had an argument it doesn't mean... it doesn't mean we can't be civilised.'

He began to turn the lights off.

'Come on,' he said. 'We'd better go up, it's late.'

The two men walked upstairs and parted at the door to the spare room. They didn't shake hands, as had always been their custom at the end of an evening, just exchanged the curtest of nods. They were friends no longer, and they both knew it.

Milne closed the door behind him and leant against it, feeling completely wretched. He staggered toward the bed, pulling his clothes off as he went and leaving them scattered over the floor. Then he lifted the bedspread and slipped his body underneath, vowing to himself that he'd rise early and leave the house before his hosts were even awake. He'd set an alarm on his phone for four or five, and that'd be it. Gone, never to return.

He smiled to think of the note he intended leaving for Bennett:

I'm sorry you feel the way you do, he would write, *but it's just the typical reaction of a talentless no-hoper who's spent his whole life sat on his arse, daydreaming, and blaming everyone else for his lack of achievement.*

He laughed to himself at how those words would hit home, and then the mists of drunken sleep began to crowd in around his mind, and he passed out.

A little later, Milne was roused from the depths of sleep by loud, angry voices. As he came nearer to consciousness he recognised them as Bennett and Debbie. My God, he thought, don't they *ever* stop arguing? Even as the thought formed in his mind, the voices did stop. He turned on to his side and dozed off again for a few minutes only to be woken once more.

By a woman's scream, swiftly silenced.

Milne sat up in a hurry. A second later the alcohol-spiked blood raced into his head creating a hiatus of pain behind his eyes and at the crown of his skull.

Jesus, what the hell's going on, he wondered, hand to throbbing head. What now?

Then the bedroom door was suddenly kicked open, making Milne jump. He reached for the bedside lamp and flicked it on, squinting at the sudden light. Bennett was standing in the doorway, stripped to the waist, with an expression of pure hatred on his face. He was covered in deep red blood. He threw something round and heavy across the room and it bounced and rolled on the bed, ending up between Milne's legs.

Milne looked down at Debbie Bennett's severed head, at the ragged tear an inch below the chin where it had been sliced from her neck. The blood was still oozing out of her veins and it quickly soaked into the bedspread. He could feel it seeping through the material and running down the insides of his naked thighs.

'Why don't you put *this* in your next film?' Bennett hissed viciously. 'Take it with my blessing, you thieving, cheating bastard!' He slammed the door behind him as he left the room.

Milne sat in the blood-wet bed shaking with fear. Long minutes passed and still Bennett didn't reappear, as Milne feared that he might. He looked down at Debbie's dead face, at her slack mouth full of foam and blood, and her dead, open eyes, the nerves in the lids above and below still quivering slightly.

'You know something,' Milne told himself quietly. 'I know *exactly* how I'd shoot this...'

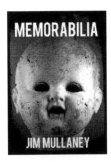

The idea for this story came from the discovery of a mouldy old autograph book in a junk shop many years ago. At first the book appeared to be entirely unused, but when I got it home and looked closer, I saw that several poems had been written in it...but by who, and when, and why did it feel so very creepy? Was it a haunted book? Put it this way – I no longer have it in my possession.

Robyn Whitford carried the tea tray through into his study and set it down carefully on the occasional table by the side of his beloved armchair. Both deep and astonishingly comfortable, the chair was a bespoke piece of furniture he'd had made just after his wife and he had first moved into the house, and no-one else had ever rested in its soothing grasp. Not even his wife – now his ex-wife, of course. It was, in every sense, his, and that's just the way he liked it.

He looked around his cosy study and smiled. He felt secure in here, completely safe and completely happy, with his book-lined shelves, and his small pieces of objet d'art, and his antique writing desk with its quills and its ink-pot with the silver lid. With his carpet footstool, and his marble fireplace. With his treasured books.

Outside the window the short day was already dying, and the pale blue light of winter grew dimmer and then dimmer still until the night was born from the cold ashes of the day. It was bitterly cold outside, and he could see fresh flakes of snow falling against the window panes, sticking to the glass for a few moments before reluctantly sliding away. He moved to the window and looked down into the garden, two floors below.

The snow was settling all right, just as the TV weatherman had predicted. In fact, if it continued to fall at this rate overnight he'd have to pay somebody to clear the drive in the morning and dig a path to the gate. Some children, perhaps, on their seasonal holiday, or maybe an unemployed person with empty pockets and a shovel would ring his doorbell and offer to do it all for a few pounds.

He couldn't possibly do it himself. He'd been fifty-seven on his birthday a few months ago, and while the task of shovelling a large amount of snow certainly wasn't physically beyond him, mentally and spiritually it was no longer a job that he would easily force himself to endure. And anyway, somebody would come to help him out. They usually did if he waited long enough... and if he paid them well enough, of course.

He closed his red velvet curtains against the darkening view of Dulwich Park and the invading winter that had come to conquer it. Then he turned and faced the room with his back to the covered window and was delighted by what he saw. The fire that he had started before he'd taken his evening bath was now well under way, a smouldering, flickering inferno, the coals glowing restfully, all oranges and reds. It illuminated the study almost as well as the standard lamp, poised beside his armchair like a faithful dog.

The world that Whitford had created for himself in this room was everything that he could possibly have wanted. It was beautiful, it was comfortable, and just spending time here eased his soul and sheltered him from harm. So different from when he'd first bought the house. Back then this room had been a playroom for children. Or at least, that's what it appeared to have been once, a very long time before.

When he'd moved in it had only been the shell of a playroom, with the style of the faded wallpaper alone betraying the fact. Its renovation had been an expensive piece of work, all the fitted oaken shelves being as bespoke as his armchair, but the money didn't matter at all. The house as it had stood had been worth more than he'd paid for it. God alone knew what it was worth at today's ridiculously inflated prices.

Whitford went to warm his hands before the fire, his mind spinning backwards in time. The price of a house wasn't something that he'd ever have thought about anyway. He had never had any troubles with regard to finance. His father had died when Whitford was twenty-three years old, and as the only child of his parents' union, he had inherited the bulk of the estate. His Mother, a cold woman toward the end of her own life, had been wealthy in her own right and upon her husband's death had immediately moved back to her family's ancestral home in Sussex. She hadn't seemed too surprised or upset when her son hadn't accompanied her.

After a brief spate of hedonism, prompted by his sudden affluence, he'd settled down to a comfortable bachelor existence in a large suite of rooms in St. John's Wood. He'd spent his time at parties, at race-courses, in the clubs of gentlemen, and in the homes of friends. It had been a pleasant, leisurely life, full of colour and the kind of adventures that rich young men could afford both at home and abroad. He'd lived that way for many years, until he'd eventually met the woman who was to become his wife.

Joyce was the first woman Whitford had ever formed a lengthy relationship with, and unfortunately his lack of experience had told. Once they'd moved into their new home together in Dulwich Village he'd found that he couldn't deal with the claustrophobic atmosphere marriage had brought into his life. He'd simply not been used to living with other people anymore, or accommodating another person's needs, insecurities and passions. Neither he nor his wife had any kind of occupation, never having had any need to work for a living. Nor did they practice any particular time-consuming hobby or pastime, and so they were together twenty-four hours a day, looking at the walls, looking at each other, and finding the experience wanting. Perhaps things might all have been different if they could have had children. But they couldn't.

Eventually he'd decided that he couldn't handle the marriage at all. Divorce was, of course, out of the question − the Whitfords did *not* get divorced − and consequently he had decided to find for himself a distraction, a barrier, through which he could regain the privacy he needed.

He had discovered one surprisingly quickly.

Whitford walked across to the study door and closed it on the rest of the house, as he had done almost every day during the vast majority of his marriage. As he had continued to do during the seven years following Joyce's defection and the divorce she had forced upon him, and all the way up to the present day.

This study, this had been his barrier against a world he had consciously decided to turn his back on. He had designed its features and had overseen its construction. He had stocked it with the sort of things that could hold his attention and interest. Joyce had had the rest of the house to do with as she wished – for a very long time, that had been *her* escape – but the study had always been completely and irredeemably his.

Joyce had been scathing on the subject, accusing him not only of living in the past, which would have been bad enough, but of living in a past that wasn't even *his*. But Joyce didn't understand. If she had, the lack of children might not have mattered so much.

Over the years Whitford had filled the many shelves with hundreds and hundreds of books, not one of them new. These were books he had gathered from charity shops and junkshops, jumble sales and antiquarian fairs. He sought out books with a history, books that had inscriptions written on the title page, *To my darling wife, with all my love*, or *To my beloved daughter, with the fond hope that...* or even just *This book belongs to...* if the book was interesting enough. He prized those rare finds, books that concealed photographs of absolute strangers still trapped between the pages, personal bookmarks pressed like summer flowers and then forgotten, lost. Were the photographs of boy or of girl there by accident? Or were they placed there so that they lay pressed against some relevant passage, a pertinent line or two of poetry or prose, casting light on the mysteries of love or loss, particularly meaningful to these unknown lovers from the past?

He pondered over such riddles constantly. He loved them.

These were the distractions that Whitford had busied himself with. The distractions he had continued to busy himself with throughout the years. The random collection of Life's lost and abandoned memorabilia had become his life's work, and his sole joy.

Even now that he had lived alone for so long it was still his barrier against the real world, an environment he found it increasingly hard to bear. A barrier against the starvation and the violence and the crime, the impending disintegration of society, and against the screaming jet-liners, the foreign accents and faces in every walk of life, and the suicide bombers and the endless run of bloody, unwinnable wars, the harsh world outside his study and outside the dwindling number of temples to the past where he found his treasures.

He knew that it was morbid to think this way, but sometimes he felt that he would die here in his study. He could picture himself quietly passing away, surrounded by the past, and being finally at peace.

Content. He thought that it would be easy, when his time came, to take his last breath and to die here, among the dead.

Whitford finally eased himself down in his armchair and poured himself a cup of tea from the large, wool-muffled pot on the tray. He added a heaped teaspoonful of white sugar and gathered up a hot and spongy slice of toast, a few small yellow islands on its dark surface the only trace of what had been a thick layer of butter. With his mouth full of the toast, he licked the grease away as it ran down his fingers and across his wrist. Then he reached for another slice.

As he munched his way through his supper he kept his eyes steadily on his latest purchases. They were stacked up on the mantelpiece, a shabby triumvirate of ill-kempt volumes which to Whitford's mind seemed to smile at him and sparkle in a manner that was decidedly friendly. He smiled back at them. He knew how much they'd appreciated being saved.

Earlier in the day he had called on an old friend who lived in Streatham Vale, about twenty to thirty minutes drive away from his own home, and there he had passed away a few idle hours, chatting. When he'd left he had taken to driving around the streets, as was his habit whenever he visited an area he had grown unfamiliar with.

It was during this ramble that he'd chanced to drive down Mitcham Lane, past the stone wall of a railway bridge decorated with a piece of graffiti, the meaning of which eluded him entirely. He'd struggled for a moment with the task, but then simply given up, thinking how out of touch he must be with the rest of humanity if even a simple piece of graffiti puzzled him now. He found that the idea of losing touch like that had its own special appeal.

However, as he had progressed along the road, this and all his other trivial thoughts, had flown from his mind, like homing pigeons that lived elsewhere. For there, nestled in the middle of a short parade of local high-street shops, was one of the oases at which he slaked his spiritual thirst: an honest-to-goodness junk shop.

It had taken only moments to park his car and walk back to the parade. Once inside the shop he was both at home and lost. *Everything* called to him. Every tattered book, every mildewed chair, every cracked china ornament, they all had stories to tell him, but he had long ago learned to discriminate between the genuinely interesting and the also-rans.

At the end of an hour's leisurely exploration, he had taken his leave of the shop with three wonderful prizes from amongst the many.

And now they waited for him on the mantelpiece.

Whitford wiped his hands clean of butter and crumbs, eager to examine the books more leisurely. The casual but intuitive glance he'd given them earlier in the shop had faded slightly from his memory and he wanted to check that he hadn't been misled by their surface attraction. He put his tea-cup down after a final sip, rose from his seat, and approached the fireplace.

Weighing them, mentally as well as physically, he took the books from the mantle with his gentle hands and returned to the armchair. The first book he'd chosen was *The Best American Short Stories of*

1945, a hardback edition originally from the United States. It had been edited by someone named Martha Foley, and from the dust jacket it boasted "Thirty-one outstanding stories by such distinguished writers as Gladys Schmitt, Leane Zugsmith, Isaac Rosenfeld and Jessamyn West". The only one of these authors Whitford had ever heard of was West, and mostly because of the trivia that she had been taught Sunday School lessons by the father of Richard Nixon, to whom she was a second cousin.

There were many more such outstanding writers named inside and he was sure that he would derive much pleasure from reading their stories and wondering where their distinguished lives had taken them. He didn't really want to know the truth about these obscure authors, but the idea of merely guessing was, as always, irresistible.

Whitford's second find was a thick and heavy British hardback entitled, *Odhams Encyclopaedia of Cookery, Illustrated*, which dated, he guessed, from the early Fifties. The tome was riddled throughout with early advertisements for kitchen and cooking products which looked naive to say the least:

"Regal full cream evaporated milk! Federation Flour - for all your baking! Kitchen Hint! Re-plate worn Cutlery, Taps etc. with Cromit, The Wonder Powder!"

Each campaign was liberally swathed in exclamation marks and gloriously hapless by today's sophisticated standards.

The other thing about this book that had caught his eye was the way the corners of many of the pages had been folded back, as if to create a method of quickly finding those favourite recipes, or perhaps those relegated to that once yearly 'special occasion', the birthday or the wedding anniversary.

With the recipes for such delicacies as *Duck Montmorency* and *Court Bouillon a La Creole* at his fingertips, he could now see himself and the characters he created from the storehouse of memories about him, feasting at immense and elaborate banquets all day and every day.

He was very pleased with his choice of books so far. Detail was becoming a more important ingredient as his armchair reconstruction of peoples' lives from the bric-a-brac of their existence became more complex and practised.

Detail from which his mind's eye could take whatever appealed and rearrange it to his ultimate satisfaction.

The best find, quite naturally, Whitford had saved until last. It was a very old pocket sized autograph book. Bound in grainy black leather well worn around the edges, it had the word *Autographs* written across its surface in a handwritten style in gold leaf.

He'd found it at the bottom of a cardboard box, under some rusty old tools and an egg-whisk, and as he'd first flicked through the book he'd thought that it had been completely unused - except that one of the pages had been cut out. But when he'd looked a little more carefully, he had discovered that there *was* a single entry.

But it wasn't an autograph, it was a poem:

Always there is seed being sown silently and unseen, and everywhere there comes sweet flowers without our foresight or labour.

We reap what we sow, but nature has love over and above that justice, and gives us shadow and blossom and fruit that spring from no planting of ours.

The poem, credited to George Eliot and written in dark blue ink in a flowing hand, had been entered and signed by a girl named Thelma and dated August 6th 1939. Whitford had been delighted with this find and had bought the book immediately at the price of 20p.

Another bargain for his collection.

Now Whitford shifted into a slightly more comfortable position in his armchair. The heat from the fire was pleasantly hot on his legs, protecting him from the chill of the night. He turned to the page with the poem, stifled a yawn, and then read it aloud, his voice low and yet strong, deeply confident of his own world and his place in it.

When he had finished reading, he stared at the name and the date. *Thelma. August 1939.* He tried to imagine the girl who had written it, tried to imagine what she had looked like and where she'd lived, and why she had copied down that particular passage at that particular moment in time, less than one full month away from the start of the Second World War. He closed his eyes and concentrated. Thelma.

Thelma.

There she was...

He could see her quite clearly now. His flight of imagination seemed to be spectacular this evening. Thelma sat on a padded window seat below tall, lead-latticed windows through which the sun bounced, emphasising the lustre of her long auburn hair and freckling her light, cool skin. And she was a woman, not a girl. The fact seemed to thrill Whitford somehow.

Beyond the window was a large garden, golden in the sunlight and resplendent with summer flowers and trees dripping with blossom – the calm before the storm soon to engulf the world. A large orange cat picked its way through a flower bed, patiently following the erratic flight of a cabbage white, an evil intent smouldering in its eyes, like an omen of things to come.

Thelma had the autograph book resting on a cushion in her lap and was signing her name below the poem. She finished writing, then laid her pen by the side of the ink-pot on the window sill and began to blow gently on the page, her rosy lips almost trembling. When she was satisfied that the ink had dried, she held the book up to the light from the window and began to read it aloud, just as Whitford had, her lovely hazel eyes following the words, her sweet voice clear and pure.

When she finished the reading she seemed to fall into a deep reverie, her head hanging, the delicate fingers of one hand picking at a loose thread on the cushion. She was far away. With some young man already called away and press-ganged into uniform, perhaps? More than a friend? More than a relative? A lover?

Whitford sighed and rubbed his eyes. He was intrigued, but beginning to be very tired, and he decided that very soon he was going to take a nap.

But first he needed a little more for his subconscious mind to work with and he flicked through the small book's pages again, hoping for some other detail to fan his creative flame until it blazed the way he knew that it could. He knew that he was probably wasting his time, but sometimes it was surprising what a second look could rev...

What was that? Whitford asked himself suddenly. Wasn't it...

He caught his breath.

He had found another entry:

> *Love to make you happy*
> *Health to make you blest*
> *That is all I wish you*
> *Leave to God the rest*

This, according to the date alongside it, had been written on Christmas Eve of the year 1920 by someone named Florrie. *1920*. Almost nineteen years before Thelma's entry. The quality of the handwriting, and also the simplicity of the rhyme, seemed to indicate that it had been written by quite a young girl.

Whitford was so excited by this discovery that despite his fatigue he began to search through the entire book once more, page by page this time, making sure that none were stuck together and being sure to check both sides.

By the time he had reached the last page of the book he had found two more entries.

These last two were also poetry, and, he suspected, also quotations, although they weren't credited or marked as such. The passages had been entered by two more girls, and the only thing that he could initially tell about them from their handwriting, or from the works they had chosen, was that they were both younger than Thelma and older than Florrie.

Their names were Alice and Laura.

Whitford held the autograph book clasped tightly in his hands and closed his eyes. He had not been disappointed. In fact, the book had exceeded all his hopes for it. He stretched out his feet before him and relaxed his whole body. Already he could feel the waves of sleep washing over him. He really did need that nap, even if it was just for half an hour. Then he was sure that he'd be able to carry on until morning began to reach him through the gap in the curtains.

And in the meantime, as he slept, perhaps he would dream of the girls, the former owners of the autograph book.

Yes, he wanted to dream about the girls.

About Alice and Laura and Florrie and Thelma.

The sisters...

That's what they were, he suddenly realised.

Sisters.

A sharp arthritic pain in his left shoulder made Whitford realise that he was waking up, and that the fast-falling images which froze for a moment before his eyes and then passed on were his dreams fading away. He caught the last few, seeing them, and recognising them, as they occurred.

An irritating game which amused and yet annoyed. A smile. A laughter that he could see and feel.

He was sluggishly awake now but hadn't yet opened his eyes. He didn't know how long he'd slept or even what time it was, and he didn't care. He was too preoccupied with trying to remember the whole of his dream so that he could lock it into his mind as a scene before he lost it altogether.

He would quickly forget if he didn't make the effort now.

Unconsciously he reached out for the cup at his side and blindly brought it to his lips. There was still a little tea in the cup. It was cold but he drank it down anyway, to take the taste of his sleep away, and then held the cup pensively in his lap.

Whitford remembered all that happened in his dream, but not at all *why* it had happened. The first thing he'd known was that he was in the garden he had imagined earlier, only now there were three other people there. It was the children, the girls who had written in the autograph book. The sisters — well, three of the four, anyway — and they were dressed in white summer dresses as timeless as summer itself.

The smallest of the girls had walked up to him, a snub-nosed, ginger-headed child. She'd bobbed a curtsy, and then introduced herself as Florrie, aged ten. She'd curtsied again at the end of this announcement and then stepped back for a second girl to approach him. This one was an older specimen and her curtsy had been brief and to the point, but her ready smile had more than made up for that. She was Laura, she'd said, and she was fifteen.

The final girl had hardly curtsied at all, but she'd nodded her head in a more or less amiable way and it would have been impossible for Whitford to miss the humour that played in those bright eyes of hers. He'd bowed to her as gravely as he could and she had broken into a fit of giggles before introducing herself as Alice. She was thirteen years old.

They were all beautiful, beautiful children.

But where was the fourth sister? Where was Thelma, and why, Whitford had suddenly wondered, even in the midst of this curious dream, did there seem to be such a large discrepancy between the sisters' ages? Thelma had seemed to be in her late twenties when he'd imagined her, and that was twice the age of the others. Was there a difference now that he was dreaming?

He'd looked back toward the house, a large, moss-covered country affair, and spotted the windows of the window seat, and the back of its occupant - Thelma. She was writing in the autograph book once more. Either that or she was living then, in that dream, the moment he had imagined for her earlier. It was rather confusing.

He'd begun to walk toward the window so that he could speak with her, but had been hampered by the younger sisters as they'd insisted upon dancing around and around him, singing a little song among themselves and getting under his feet.

By the time they had finished their dance, their charming but irritating game, Thelma had finished writing. She'd raised the book up to her lips, and when she'd blown on the ink to dry it, Whitford had felt the first of the pain in his shoulder and begun to wake up.

Fully awake now, Whitford sat up in his chair. His eyes were still closed as he pondered over the details of his dream and congratulated himself for remembering it so well. Time to begin again, he thought, and opened his eyes.

He screamed at what he saw before him. The tea-cup fell from his hands to the floor and broke as his arms jerked convulsively.

On the mantelpiece above the glowing fire, three spectres sat side by side, swinging their legs and staring at him. He knew who they were. He had met them in a dream and now they were here in reality.

This wasn't a dream. Whitford knew it, and he was terrified. The pain in his shoulder suddenly seemed to intensify and to flow down his arm and begin to seep into his chest.

'Hello, Robyn,' Laura said to him brightly. Her voice actually hurt his ears but he couldn't raise his hands to cover them. 'I think he's surprised to see us, Alice.'

Alice nodded. 'Yes. I think he is. I don't see why, though. He's been inviting us all day.'

Whitford sat in absolute silence, staring at the girls, the ghosts, the... things. Each was now dressed in an old-fashioned linen nightdress that stretched from neck to ankle. Their bare little feet dangled perilously close to the rising heat from the fire, but it didn't seem to worry them. He looked closer at their faces and tried to work out what it was that had changed about them.

Surely their faces were gaunter, their skin pallid, and even more sallow than before?

'Well?' Florrie said, petulantly. 'Aren't you going to speak to us? We've come all the way here just to see you, you know.'

Whitford swallowed and cleared his throat. 'Where have you come from?' he asked, his voice uneven.

Florrie's face dropped for an instant, she looked wary, as if she had been tempted to reveal a secret. Then she turned to her sisters for support. Alice smiled at her, nodding, and watched her sister's face recompose itself. Then she turned to Whitford and let her manic, sparkling eyes burn into his. He twisted his head to one side so that he wouldn't have to look.

'From your garden, of course,' Alice said, grinning. The other two sisters began to smile also.

'Then why aren't you there now?' he asked without turning back. He was almost crying. 'Why don't you go back? Why don't you go away?'

'Because it was *your* garden, you silly!' she replied. 'You made it for us, just as you made the white dresses and the house. They don't belong to us. We don't belong to them.'

'Then where do you belong?'

The three girls began to laugh at his question. A gleeful laughter that shook the room and seemed to tear at Whitford's skin and burn his eyes.

'Haven't you guessed?' Alice asked as the laughter died.

She pointed down at his lap. The autograph book lay between his leg and the arm of the chair.

'There,' she said. *'There.'*

Whitford managed to touch the book with his shaking right hand. It was all he could do, the pain in his shoulder, arm and chest was now paralysing. 'From here? But it's only a book.'

The sisters laughed at him again, leaning together, their hands held over their mouths.

'It isn't a *book*,' Laura said, giggling through her fingers. 'It's a *demon*!'

Whitford stared at her. He shook his head. 'No...'

'I found it under my pillow on Christmas Eve,' Florrie whispered, leaning forward conspiratorially. The glow from the fire highlighted the red in her hair, throwing her thin, lineless face into shadow. 'I thought it was an early Christmas present from Mummy and I wrote a poem in it in my best handwriting to show her in the morning. I wanted to make her happy again, because she'd been so sad since Daddy died. But then, when I went to sleep, the demon that lives in the book came and took me.'

'I don't believe it,' Whitford said, shaking his head more fiercely.

'But it's true!' Florrie squealed. 'It really is!'

'Oh, he believes,' Alice said. 'He just doesn't *want* to.'

'And then later on,' Florrie continued, 'after they buried my body, Laura wrote in the book in memory of me, and then I came and took her.'

'And when Alice wrote something else there for me,' Laura added, 'it was *my* turn to take *her*.'

Whitford looked at the three in horror. They were right. He didn't want to believe – but he did.

'And then I had *such* a long wait,' Alice told him, pouting. 'Because clever-clever Thelma had guessed what the book was. She *knew* what the demon had done. She *knew* that it was a collector of souls.'

'She almost asked us to come for her once,' Florrie said. 'When Mummy died of sorrow for us, and she was left all alone in the world, an orphan. But she cut the page out before she'd finished writing.'

'And so we had to wait until she'd grown up,' Alice said regretfully. 'Until she'd tired of life. Until she'd been hurt too much. Until she didn't care anymore.' She smiled suddenly. 'Eventually she wrote her farewell to the world, knowing that we would finally be reunited. Then I took her.'

Whitford shifted in his seat. The pain was growing worse, and yet he was beginning to feel distinctly chilly, despite his distress and the heat from the fire. The veins on the backs of his hands were distended and blue.

'And where is...' he began, and then stopped, fear silencing him. A hand had fallen on his shoulder.

He managed to turn his head to see Thelma walking around the armchair, her shapely body wrapped in a clinging nightdress of satin and lace. But she was not the Thelma he had imagined.

Her hair was the same pretty shade of auburn, her eyes the same mixture of brown and green, but gone was the sweetness and purity he had attributed to her. In their place was a wantonness, an unnatural sensuality in her every movement. Her hand left his shoulder and he felt a strange sense of loss.

Thelma walked across to the fireplace and kissed each of her sisters in turn, first one cheek then the other, and then she turned to face Whitford.

'I've waited a long time for you, Robyn,' she said. 'And now at last it's *my* turn.'

'No!' Whitford shouted. He tried to get out of his chair, but he found himself unable to rise. The pain doubled, his chest caught in a vice. 'But you can't take me,' he told them desperately. 'I haven't written in the book!'

Thelma smiled at him. 'Take another look,' she said. Even in his terror he found her voice arousing.

He felt his hands being released from the paralysis and he opened the autograph book completely at random, and somehow found a page with an inscription that he hadn't seen before. It was more poetry, and in a different hand to the others:

The day returns and brings us the petty round of irritating concerns and duties.

Help us to play the wan; help us to perform them with daughters and kind faces; let cheerfulness abound with industry.

Give us to go blithely on our business all this day; bringing us to our resting beds weary and content and grant us in the end the gift of sleep.

The passage was one that Whitford knew well - it was by Robert Louis Stevenson, and he had several copies of it in various collections of verse. And the entry *was* in his handwriting, the ink still damp enough to smudge slightly against his thumb.

With a great effort he managed to twist around so that he could see the writing desk. The silver lid was off the inkpot and one of the quills lay by its side, recently used. He'd written it in his sleep. Somehow they had made him write it in his sleep.

Whitford moaned aloud as he slumped back in his chair, no longer possessing the strength with which to fight the power that sought to restrain him or the raging agony now building to a crescendo in his chest. He was shaking with fear and terror and pain and there were tears in his eyes. He looked at Thelma.

'I don't want to die,' he said.

Thelma stepped forward.

'Of course you do, Robyn,' she answered. 'You've been praying for it all night. "...*and grant us in the end the gift of sleep...*" Remember? And now I've come to take you.'

She took the autograph book from his hand, raised it to her lips and then blew on the ink for a moment, until it had completely dried. Then she licked her lips, as though in anticipation. Whitford quivered at the sight.

Thelma closed the book and set it aside as she sat on his lap, wrapping her long pale arms about his neck. As her weightless body rested upon his, he felt at once terrified and bizarrely excited. He held his breath as she pulled herself closer to him, her delicate breasts held tight against his burning chest. Over her shoulder he saw the three younger sisters watching them intently with expressions of indescribable hunger.

'Sisters,' Thelma said softly. 'Our family grows...' She placed a hand under Whitford's chin and pushed his head back until it faced her own.

'And now,' she said to Whitford's soul. 'A little kiss, if you please.'

She pressed her cold lips against his. He tried to twist his head away but she was far stronger than he. Her tongue broke through the feeble barrier of his lips and teeth and he could feel his commitment to life fading away, as his strength had. The pain first eased and then erased. Then he felt nothing at all. No pain and no terror, but also no warmth and no love.

Out of the corners of his eyes he could see his study, his world, and his life disappearing as it was taken out of him through Thelma's kiss. The first and last kiss of that kind she would ever give him, for soon he would be her brother.

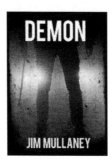

I'll make no bones about it, this is a nasty, tasteless little story, and not a trace of the supernatural about it, either. No excuses. But at its core, 'Demon' is really about destructive patterns of behaviour, about unbroken cycles of abuse, and violence begetting violence... and a fairly literal interpretation of biblical justice.

A dream, he thought. How curious.

Peter Wainwright did not dream. Ever. It was one of the rules of his personal philosophy, one of his commandments. *I shall not dream.* His commandments had been set in place and strictly observed ever since his ninth birthday, and now he was within three days of being thirty-nine. Not that he had ever acknowledged any birthday after his ninth. Another commandment.

The dream... Well, it wasn't as though anything much was happening. But still he didn't like it, because all dreams, at their dark hearts, were nightmares. Why else the commandment?

The dream was very simple. He was sitting on a chair that felt like a dining chair, and he seemed to be tied to it. He couldn't be absolutely sure of either of these details because he was in complete darkness, a little bit cold and a little bit numb. He also felt groggy, and the back of his head hurt. He could hear traffic sounds, but at a distance, and closer, much closer, he could hear somebody breathing heavily, although possibly he was only hearing himself. He could smell dust and oil.

Truth be told, it was a *stupid* dream, and he was vaguely disappointed in himself. He had broken one of his own commandments for this nonsense?

But stupid or not, Wainwright could not seem to will the dream away. He couldn't seem to force himself to wake up, either, and if there was one thing he was good at, waking up was it. Usually he woke up between six and ten times each night, each time bathed in the sour, goaty reek of his own sweat.

He had never been tempted to consult a doctor about this oddity in his sleep pattern. To him it was normal. It was the way he had always been, ever since he was nine. And anyway, what could a doctor do except stuff him full of pills, or send him to a pointless sleep disorders clinic, or place him into the clutches of a psychiatrist. Wainwright did not want to risk the attentions of a psychiatrist. Everyone knew how they twisted everything you said, how they saw messages in dreams and made patterns out of the past like shaman making prophecies out of a mess of chicken guts.

Suddenly there was a scraping noise in front of him, and he raised his head in alarm. The noise had sounded like the sole of a shoe, shuffling on a gritty floor. Slight though it had been, the sound seemed to have generated an echo. Wainwright's ankles felt less tightly bound than the rest of him, so he experimented by moving his feet. They made exactly the same scraping noise, and the same shallow echo.

'So, you're awake at last,' a deep male voice intoned in the darkness.

Now Wainwright was scared. He wasn't quite sure why. Was it the deep male voice, speaking out of darkness, or was it the specific words that were spoken? Was it both elements in conjunction? Were they frightening because they evoked in him a powerful sense of déjà vu? He desperately wanted to wake up.

More scraping noises, now becoming definite footsteps. Then a sharp click and the air was full of fire. No, not fire, just light, an electric light, but after so long in total darkness it burnt Wainwright's eyes. Behind his eyelids the image of an electric bulb was imprinted on his retinas.

'Open your eyes,' the voice said.

Wainwright had no intention of opening his eyes. He knew the sort of thing that happened in dreams, even though he never normally suffered from them himself.

'No, it isn't,' the voice said. 'And you won't.'

Wainwright realised he'd been whispering to himself in a curious childlike falsetto, 'It's a dream, it's a dream, it's a dream, wake up, wake up, wake up...'

'Do you want to know where you are?'

Wainwright hesitated, unwilling to interact with the dream, but then he just nodded.

'Good. You're in the Court of Retribution, the Home of True Justice. You're incarcerated in HM

Prison Eye-for-an-Eye, Miles from Hope. Wainwright, Peter Edward, you're finished.'

That voice, he thought. I *know* that voice. And with that recognition came the chill realisation that this was not a dream, after all. His last moment of consciousness came back to him in a rush, and they were not taken up with his usual bedtime routine, his bedtime commandments. The purging, the bathing, the restraints.

He remembered a knock at the back door of his house, he remembered leaving the living room, turning on the light in the kitchen and discovering that the back door, which he always kept firmly locked, was standing ajar. He remembered the shock that had all but petrified him, throwing his normally ordered thoughts into such chaos that he never heard the footsteps coming up behind him, and he only realised that someone else was there as a shadow at the periphery of his vision streaked down towards the back of his head.

This was no dream. This was reality.

Okay, then. He was very good at coping with reality. He knew all the rules. They weren't in the same league as his own commandments, but he knew them. He knew how the world worked. He wasn't scared of anyone alive.

Wainwright opened his eyes, squinting against the angle-poise lamp aimed straight into his face. Then he saw the outline of a man lurking behind it. The man's voice was very familiar. There had been a three-month period last year when he'd had to listen to it each and every day, sometimes *all* day.

'Detective Inspector Murray,' he said calmly. His sharp, no-nonsense voice echoed impressively, just as though he wasn't tied to a chair. 'Why don't you take that lamp out of my face and tell me what the hell you think you're playing at.'

The shadow behind the light moved a little, and the lamp was pointed downwards, the glare fading. He saw that it stood on a large upturned packing crate, beside which stood a large old briefcase, much battered and scuffed. The same case that Murray had brought with him to the interview room, day after day after day. The spill of light around the crate was strong enough for Wainwright to see that the lamp was being run off a car battery on the floor. The floor was of rough concrete, liver-spotted with oily patches. The light wasn't strong enough to reveal a wall. He remembered the echoes, given off by the smallest sounds. Big place, he thought. Factory, maybe.

'Where are we?' he asked.

DI Murray, his long face dark with greying stubble, remained at the other side of the light. 'The old Forbut engineering works, in Sharples.'

Wainwright took this in. 'I thought it had been demolished.'

'Next week.'

Wainwright knew that the Forbut building was at the centre of a large derelict industrial estate in the Sharples area, long abandoned and scheduled for demolition to make way for a new shopping and housing complex. Murray had lost it, big time, bringing him here – trying to scare him, no doubt.

Wainwright felt as though he had developed x-ray vision. Inside the briefcase he could see a tape-recorder, a writing pad, and a pen. He could see inside Murray's head, too. He could see the image of a signed confession. He managed not to laugh out loud.

'This's going to lose you your job, Murray – you know that, don't you?'

Murray didn't reply, just continued to stare at Wainwright with undiminished loathing. Wainwright had had to put up with that self-same stare for three whole months. It had made him sick, but he'd handled it. He could handle it now.

'Inspector, you had not one single shred of hard evidence on me,' he said calmly. 'Nothing to connect me to those people or to the activities they indulged in. Nothing to connect me to the boy or the crime itself. It was all circumstantial. That's why it never made it to court.'

'You killed him,' Murray barked. 'You were there. You organised it, you abducted him, you were the ringleader.'

Wainwright shook his head, a small sad smile on his lips.

Poor little Bryan Brownlow, stolen off a street-corner on his way back from a sweet shop half a mile from his parents' home, driven to an unknown location, raped, tortured, and finally suffocated and dismembered by three masked and body-painted 'demons'. All of this recorded live by two digital cameras and later edited to professional standards. HD downloads of the production had been offered for sale at a grand apiece. Entitled *Demon Party*, over five thousand orders had been placed by perverts from all over the world, the money disappearing through God knows how many secret internet crevices to bank accounts in international tax havens.

'I understand how this case must have got under your skin, Inspector.' Wainwright's voice was warm and sympathetic and reasonable. 'I can even understand why I was briefly considered to be a suspect.'

Wainwright was a one-man-band video production company, specialising in event documentation. Conferences, AGMs, wedding videos, birthdays, Christenings, Confirmations, and Bar Mitzvahs. The two men, known paedophiles, found in possession of DVDs of *Demon Party* had given police the names of two cameramen who were immediately arrested, and all four of them identified Wainwright not only as the provider of the equipment, but also as the third 'demon' in the film.

Wainwright denied it all, claiming the four men were business rivals, attempting to drag him into their depravity. Apart from the four men's testimony, the police had no other evidence to connect Wainwright to the case. A search of his business premises, stock, and equipment revealed nothing incriminating, and neither did the brutal ransacking of his home or detailed forensic examination of the hard-drives on his PC and laptop. Not one person, his four accusers aside, had anything bad to say about him. Several prominent local businessmen and politicians came out in his support.

But DI Murray, heading the investigation, had seen something off-kilter about him during the course of their many interviews. It was nothing he was able to adequately explain to his colleagues, or justify to his superiors when Wainwright began to whine about victimisation. It was nothing the CPS would have been prepared to take to court. It was an indefinable feeling. It was the unnatural calmness of the man under tough interrogation, the pat answers delivered with a punchline panache, and the knowing looks that said, *this is a game and I hold all the cards.*

Only this past week, all four paedophiles had finally been convicted and sentenced for their part in the crime. The lightest sentence was life imprisonment, with a recommended minimum of twenty-five years to be served. It was believed that the judge in the trial had been enraged by the crime's heartless poignancy. Ryan Brownlow's remains had been dumped in a reservoir where his father used to take him windsurfing. And he had been abducted on the morning of his ninth birthday.

'What exactly are you hoping to achieve with this madness?' Wainwright asked. 'I'm innocent. I swear I'm innocent.'

Murray did not reply and Wainwright shrugged, as much as he was able within the confines of his bonds.

'Okay,' he sighed. 'Let's get it over with, then you can take me to the station. Do you want to turn your tape recorder on,' he said, nodding at Murray's old briefcase, 'or is it running already?'

The DI didn't move.

'If you prefer, I'll write it down and sign it,' Wainwright said. 'Just untie me and I'll do it right now. How I participated in the death of Ryan

Brownlow, a confession by Peter Edward Wainwright.'

He smiled. *This is a game*, the smile said. I know the rules. I hold all the cards. I will be the winner. A confession obtained under these circumstances would be completely worthless.

'Come on, let's get on with–'

'I don't want a confession,' Murray said. 'I know you did it. I don't need a confession.'

Ignoring the sudden frown on Wainwright's face, the DI finally approached his briefcase and stooped to open it. He began unloading the tools, placing them in an orderly line on the top of the packing case directly under the lamplight. A hammer. A Stanley knife. Knitting needles. A lighter and a small blowtorch. Replicas of those implements used on Bryan Brownlow prior to his murder. Wainwright watched them come out, one by one. Behind his calm mask his mind had locked.

Retribution, he thought. An eye for an eye, he thought. True justice. Miles from hope. Finished.

'Take me to the station,' Wainwright said quickly. 'Take me now and I'll give my confession there. I'll give you a confession you can use, and I'll stand by it. I'll plead guilty in court.'

For the first time, Murray stepped around the packing case, his face set, and Wainwright suddenly knew that no amount of pleading would stop this from happening. Nothing would. The metallic taste of pennies in his mouth was so very familiar.

'You can't hurt me any worse than I've already been hurt,' he said.

He resolved not to beg, because it did no good. He was determined not to cry, because that only made it worse. No matter what was done to him, he wouldn't make a sound. This had always been his response to pain. It was one of his commandments.

Ever since he was nine.

This is one of a series of short stories that grew out of an abandoned long novel set in an experimental city of the near-future called Gooseberry Hill. This city had been designed to safeguard all the country's most sensitive secrets, everything from germ warfare research programmes to the custody of an alien lifeform. But unfortunately the city had been built in the worst possible location, on land that had its own, far deeper, far older secrets.

When David Lester was a boy, his father was a distant figure. In fact, all David's strongest memories of his father were actually memories of his absence. He worked all the time, and when he did not work, he was always too tired, too busy to spare his son the attention he both craved and merited. Generally, his father was a grunt in the morning, and that was it. Only after meeting Louise, the woman he would eventually marry, had David realised that a father could be something more than a mannequin you nodded to at breakfast time. A teacher, a playmate, a storyteller, and a hundred more things besides.

But a storyteller more than anything else.

As they became ever more attached during their university years, Louise would occasionally regale him with memories of the tall tales her father had made up for her when she was a young girl. When he would come home from work each evening to sweep her into his arms and blow fragrant tobacco kisses into her hairline. Between bath-time and bedtime, the time Louise had come to think of as the Magic Hour, her father would fill her mind with delightful nonsense, reams and reams of it, as though he had spent his whole working day doing little else but concoct fantastic stories to entertain his daughter at night.

Hard pushed to remember even a single magic moment let alone a daily Magic Hour, David had listened to her memories, at first disbelieving, but eventually bereft. For the first time he felt that he had missed out on something vital and miraculous during his childhood. His father had died some years before he and Louise had met and fallen in love, and his death had not left a hole in David's teenage life. At a time of life full of emotional turbulence and confusion, the passing of his father had meant very little to David. With the benefit of hindsight, and having had the blessing of seeing the world through Louise's eyes, David found that a terribly sad epitaph for a man.

Life moved on, but that sad memory of absence never left David, and he told Louise one day a year before they were married, that if they were ever to have children of their own, he would *not* be like his father. He would *not* be the distant figure. He would *not* be the nonentity whose passing caused no more than a ripple.

Three years later, David and Louise made the move to Gooseberry Hill, a so-called 'new-city' built from scratch in the middle of Wiltshire, so that David could take up his new managerial position in the R&D department at Technic-Cillson Laboratories. David had become a bio-chemist. Louise was a Secondary School English teacher. Both were young and hard-working, and the subject of starting a family had never seriously arisen, until the time when scheming Mother Nature settled the matter for them.

By the time they moved into their three-bedroom house at the eastern base of Gooseberry hill itself, the topographical landmark that had given the city its name, Louise was already six weeks pregnant, despite her daily pill. Shock and surprise were present on the occasion of that discovery, but both were short-lived, and another soon took over and took up permanent residence in their home. That emotion was joy.

Seven months later, a little early but trouble free and healthy, Harry Fredrick Lester was born. He had eyes like sapphires and hair like a baby gorilla. 'Harry' was after Louise's father, the storyteller. 'Fredrick' was after David's father, the blank, the nothing. David couldn't have cared less about naming his son after his own father, but Louise had insisted, saying that one day he *would* care. Later on, David would decide that one of the reasons he loved Louise as much as he did was because of her wise, understanding heart.

For David, facing the fact of being a father meant facing up to all the promises he had made to himself years before. But he *did* face up to them. He worked just as hard, if not harder, than his father had before him, but he allowed neither ambition nor fatigue to diminish his commitment to his young son. Every minute he was not working, he spent with Louise and Harry. He bathed, he changed, he night-fed, and he helped nurse the boy through colic and fevers, and all the other infant ailments.

And he told him stories.

It all started during the long sleepless nights of the first three months of the new life, when the grind of work and home had begun to wear him down. At three o'clock in the morning with a wailing infant in his arms for the seventh night in succession, walking and rocking, rocking and walking, David had come as close as he ever would to understanding his father's state of mind. He too craved solitude, silence, and freedom from the little Caligula who owned him body and soul, and it was in that moment of understanding that he began to forgive his father for his weakness.

It was an important moment, for more than one reason. Most importantly of all, that first small story paved the way for all those which were to follow.

Whispering sentences as they occurred to him into his son's tiny ear, he told the tale of a creature called The Nothing Man, a man who had removed himself so far from the lives of others that he had become invisible. That is until, one day, he came upon a crying baby left alone in its pram outside a small house. This invisible man, this nothing, this blank, stepped into the little garden and looked into the pram. The baby stopped shrieking immediately, and with a shock The Nothing Man realised that the baby could actually *see* him. Oddly delighted by this discovery, he began to speak to the child in soothing tones, and just the sound of his voice made the little one smile through its tears. Then, emboldened, he told it a little joke about the chicken crossing the road, and although the baby – like Harry – was far too young to understand even a single word, it seemed to laugh at him. Its tears were already drying on its fat cheeks.

Even further emboldened, The Nothing Man began to tell the baby a story about an enchanted princess, and it stared at him, rapt, throughout. But just as The Nothing Man's story ended, he was startled by a woman's angry voice. *Here, you!* the woman shouted. *What are you doing with my baby?* And The Nothing Man realised that the woman could see him now, too, that he was no longer invisible. He was not The Nothing Man, after all.

He was suddenly filled with an immense joy, and as she approached the pram, he grabbed the baby's mother and planted a quick kiss on a cheek almost as chubby as her baby's. He began to waltz her around the garden, laughing at her startled, blushing face, around and around – until the moment he realised that she wasn't blushing because a strange man was dancing her wildly through the buttercups and daisies. She was blushing for an entirely different reason.

He looked down at himself, aghast, and then ran back off to his own house, full of embarrassment. He was embarrassed because having been invisible for so long, he had got into the habit of going about entirely naked to save on laundry bills, and he was naked now.

He ran through the streets, clutching himself fore and aft, followed by the laughter of all the people he encountered along the way. But the laughter did not embitter him, as it would once have done, it merely underlined the fact that he was no longer invisible, he was no longer a nothing. And from that day forward, David finished, The Nothing Man was known about town as The *Wears* Nothing Man.

By the time the story was over, Harry was fast asleep. In all probability, David suspected that it was the comforting drone of his voice that had finally sent the little one off more than anything else. But still, it had been his first story, Harry's *and* David's, and he thought it had gone all right. After laying his son down gently in his cot and covering him, David turned to leave the room and found Louise leaning in the doorway. Obviously she had been standing there for some time and had heard nearly all of the story. She was smiling, and David felt a curious sense of embarrassment of his own. But that was quickly banished when Louise held out her hand to him and led him back to their own bedroom, and they made love together for the first time since Harry's birth.

It is a curse that happy time is quick time, although David never once in the next five years felt anything other than blessed. His career was blossoming, his marriage was becoming stronger and more satisfying day by day, and his son grew and thrived without mishap or tragedy.

Every evening David would arrive home at Ashton Close to find Harry waiting for him, usually sitting on the porch steps looking up at the eastern flank of Gooseberry Hill, which the five-year-old seemed to regard as his family's personal property.

After dinner with Louise, David and Harry would go upstairs, where David would give Harry his bath. Then they would retire to Harry's bedroom, which had a large bay window looking out on to the Hill. Then the stories would be told, as the sun lowered and the shadow of the Hill reached steadily towards their house, climbing up the wall, inch by inch, until it reached the bedroom window.

Sometimes Louise came to listen, sometimes not. Sometimes she would just sit in the kitchen downstairs with a good cup of coffee and a book, content to hear only the faint murmurings of David's voice as it carried through the otherwise golden silence of the house. It was the Magic Hour for them all.

David's repertoire had grown enormously over the five years of Harry's life. He'd adapted some of his stories from conventional fairy tales, some from books, and others from films Harry had seen. The boy had favourites he sometimes wanted to be told again and again, like *Burp − The Tuba-Playing Mouse*, or the rather less Disney-ish, *Showdown in Dog Poo Street*. But the best stories, the ones they both liked best, were those David made up on the spot from nothing more than the germ of an idea. These stories were wilder and less structured, and although they generally made less sense they were usually funnier, if sometimes, like the infamous *Dog Poo Street*, downright distasteful.

One evening, as the nightly Magic Hour drew to a close with a more or less traditional version of *Snow White*, Harry mumbled something as he was slipping into sleep. David thought it was, 'They like to listen.'

The next evening, Harry insisted that his bedroom window was to be left wide open for the story, instead of just the single notch the security latch allowed. When David asked why, Harry said the same thing: 'They like to listen.'

'*Who* like to listen, Harry?'

'The Hill People.' The boy frowned at his father quizzically. 'You know about the Hill People, don't you, Daddy?'

'Of course,' David lied. 'But I didn't know that they listened to my stories.'

'They do, all the time. They don't like it when you stop.'

'Well, I have to stop when you go to sleep, Harry.'

'I know. But they don't like it.

David smiled, trying to disguise the odd sense of unease the conversation had awoken in him. 'Tell you what, kiddo, know what I'm going to do? I'm going to try to make the stories even better – then the Hill People won't have anything to complain about, will they?'

Harry cheered and jumped forward for a hug.

That night, after the Magic Hour was over, David and Louise discussed the Hill People. Kids sometimes have imaginary friends, that's the long and the short of it, Louise said, unperturbed, before revealing that she'd had one of her own for a couple of years, a little Chinese girl called Lei. Didn't David ever have one? David was tempted to say, no, I had an imaginary father instead. But it would have been a cheap one-liner, and, in any case, most of the old animosity had almost entirely faded. He was glad now that Harry was also named after his father as well as Louise's, just as his wonderful wife had predicted.

Every evening after that the window was left open, and the Hill's shadow seemed to creep in though it with an almost physical presence. David's stories were better, as promised, and Harry would sometimes clap his hands together and say, 'They like that bit!' Sometimes he would laugh because he imagined the Hill People were laughing, and he could hear them.

After a while, Harry began to request certain stories, not because they were his favourites, but because they were the Hill People's.

The Hill People's most favourite story by far was one David called *The 'Orrible Old Ogre 'Ooo 'Opped on Oberon Orpington's Odd 'Ead*, and soon David found himself telling it two, sometimes three times a week. It was bearable for a while, because he was able to think up new twists and turns and new details to the story, and occasionally he told little side stories within the main story. But soon it seemed that he was telling the Ogre story every night, and it began to concern him.

Louise told him not to worry about it, and that he should continue to humour Harry, because kids got little obsessions like this from time to time, and then grew out of them just as quickly as they'd grown into them. Initially, David agreed. But after ten consecutive nights of the Ogre story, for the first time David was prepared to deny his son the story of his choice. He didn't like to even think of doing it, but he felt that he ought to. He didn't believe this obsession was healthy.

That evening saw a subdued bath-time, both father and son quiet, as though Harry had picked up on his father's intentions telepathically and was already downhearted. David saw the shadows of his own disappointments on his son's face, and by the time Harry was dried and in his pyjamas, a chastened David was fully prepared to tell the Ogre story yet again. He was prepared to tell it a thousand times, if need be, if it would make his son happy.

But before they settled down together on the bed, Harry walked over to the window and said in a very clear voice that sounded almost adult, 'I don't want the Ogre story tonight. I don't want the Ogre story ever again. I want something new.' Then he firmly closed the window, shutting out the coming night and the growing shadow of the Hill.

David was surprised but only too happy to oblige, and quickly fabricated a ludicrous story about a fox trying to raid a farmyard henhouse while wearing stilts.

A little while into the story, David looked at the joy and the pleasure on his son's face as Mr Fox's stilts were fixed to roller skates by mischievous chickens, and he realised something he should have seen days ago. The reason why he hadn't enjoyed telling the Ogre story all the time, despite its many comical sidetracks, was that Harry *himself* hadn't been enjoying it.

When David compared the face he saw now, one that was utterly transported by pleasure, to the one he had faced over the last week and a half, he was struck by their difference. *This* was the real storytelling smile, a genuine Magic Hour face. Not the Ogre face, a tired, bearing–up kind of smile fixed upon those little lips like a tiny mask. When a story had been really good, Harry smiled in his sleep afterward. That night, for the first time in ages, Harry smiled in his sleep.

David went downstairs to Louise afterwards. She was sitting at the kitchen table wearing one of his shirts and nothing else. The smile on her face told him that she'd heard everything.

'I told you he'd get out of it, didn't I?' she crowed.

'Yes, all right, you did,' David conceded. 'But then,' he said, leaning over her as she nursed her cup of coffee, 'if you're so smart, why aren't you wearing any clothes?'

'Just getting ready for my own Magic Hour.'

David slipped his hand inside her borrowed shirt. 'You want me to tell you a story?'

'Only if it's good and filthy.'

David dreamed in the night that he could hear Harry's voice calling him, begging him to wake up, and as he struggled out of deep, post-coital sleep, he realised that it was true. Harry stood beside the bed, his little body silhouetted against the soft glow from the nightlight on the landing.

'Harry?' David's mind was befuddled. He glanced at the bedside clock. It was after three in the morning. Beside him, Louise had stolen most of the duvet and had wrapped herself in it like a shroud. She didn't stir. 'What is it, Harry?' David whispered. 'Did you have a bad dream?'

'Daddy, come with me. I want you to do something for me.'

'Harry, it's the middle of the night.'

'Please come.'

David couldn't deny Harry anything. He eased himself out of bed, so as not to disturb his wife. 'Okay, what do you want to–'

Harry's little hand grabbed his big hand and pulled him out of the bedroom as though he weighed nothing. 'Come on, Daddy.'

'Where are we going? What do you want me to do?'

'I want the Ogre story.'

A small chill settled in David's chest. 'Harry, it's too late for stories, and anyway, haven't you had enough of that...'

David heard his own voice tapering away like a recording. As he was pulled across the landing, he'd glanced across through the open door into Harry's room. He could see his son on the bed, all the covers kicked off on to the floor. Harry was tying himself into knots in his sleep, sweating so heavily his fringe was plastered to his forehead. He was moaning, mumbling.

'...don't, please don't, I won't do it again, please don't take him, please don't take my daddy...'

David looked down at the tiny tousled head bobbing below him as it descended the staircase, pulling him along, its matching little hand a fist around his fingers.

It's a *dream*, he thought with considerable relief.

He remembered following Louise up the stairs to bed, the filthy story that never got further than the introduction before it wasn't a story anymore. Between bouts of lovemaking, he'd been sent down for supplies, coming back with a bottle of wine, a cheese-board and pickles. Lots and lots of pickles for the lady. The impromptu feast reminded them both of Louise's pregnancy cravings.

Is that what this is, David wondered. A precognitive dream? He and Louise had talked about having another baby soon, so that Harry wouldn't grow up an only child. Had she stopped taking precautions already, was a baby growing inside her now, is that why she wanted the cheese and pickles? One Harry upstairs in bed, another Harry leading him now across the darkened living room towards the entrance hall.

Were they destined to have another son?

Harry unlocked the front door and threw it open, and David felt the night chill his naked flesh. 'Harry, I can't go out there, I haven't any clothes on.'

The boy pulled him out anyway, down the porch steps and across the lawn, saying nothing. David looked up anxiously at the windows of the other houses in Ashton Close, but then remembered that this was all a dream and the fact that his penis was waving in the breeze didn't matter at all. Still, dream or not, his son was dragging him along the pavement at such a swift pace that he was out of breath.

'Harry, stop! Let's go back, I thought you wanted a story.'

'Not *a* story. *The* story.'

'The Ogre story?'

'Yessss.' Such satisfaction in that single, drawn-out word. But his voice seemed a little husky, like he was catching a cold.

'Okay,' David said. 'Let's stop here and I'll tell it to you.'

'Not here.'

Then where, David wondered. Silly question, really. Harry pulled him off the pavement, out of the Close itself, and into the trees at the base of Gooseberry Hill. David felt sharp stones and twigs under his bare feet, and thought what a very vivid dream this was turning out to be. He could easily turn this into a story for the real Harry, and if it turned out that Louise really *was* pregnant, it would make it even more special. Although...

The real Harry.

The phrase chimed in his head forbiddingly as they moved swiftly uphill, up into the darkness of the trees.

The real Harry.

David saw his son again, sweating in bed, struggling against sleep as though trying with all his might to wake. '...don't, please don't take my daddy...'

David's ankle was caught by a thorn on one of the numerous gooseberry bushes the Hill had presumably been named for, and he hissed in pain. He tried to stop but Harry seemed to sense his hesitation and began to pull him faster and faster.

The *real* Harry?

'Where...where are you taking me?' David asked, now having to fight for his breath. 'Harry?'

'To the othersss.' His husky little voice was now almost a growl.

David could no longer see anything. There was no moon and the streetlights in the Close didn't reach as far up the Hill as they now must have been. Even if the lights did reach this high, how could they hope to penetrate the compacted denseness of the trees and bushes? He realised that something had happened to Harry's hand. It seemed to have grown, moved, without every letting go. At the start of this dream journey it had been wrapped around the first three fingers of his left hand. Now the powerful grip had expanded to include not only his whole hand and wrist but most of his forearm as well. It was like being held by a giant.

He's taking me to the others, David thought. They want to hear the Ogre story. They were taking him because Harry didn't want to hear it anymore, and because he'd closed his bedroom window and shut them out. The Hill People.

'...please don't take him, I won't do it again...'

Harry wouldn't share, so *they* wouldn't share. They were taking him. The Hill People were taking him.

David tripped over a root in the dark, but the thing that was pulling him never stopped, never paused, just continued pulling him at a pace nothing human could have matched through thick tangles of gooseberry bushes full of thorns that tore bloody stripes across his skin like a thousand whips.

'Harry! Harry!'

David was bellowing but he knew he'd never be heard. He could hardly hear himself scream over the sound of the undergrowth being torn apart by the passage of the creature that had him. He felt his shoulder pop out of its socket and he hit his head on something, a rock or a tree stump, and then he was dragged through an even denser gooseberry bush that made him feel as though he'd been flayed alive.

'*Harry!*'

And then he was suddenly surrounded by a quality of silence that was almost shocking. No more trampled foliage, no snapping branches. His screams were muted, deadened. His feet, trailing behind him as he was dragged, dug furrows in soft earth. He was underground. He was actually *inside* the Hill. He was in the lair of The Hill People, where the real ogres lived, and nothing could save him now.

'Harry,' he whispered. 'Why us?'

Abruptly the thing let go of his arm and he fell, grinding to an abrasive stop. His breath was ragged, but not as ragged as the breathing of the creatures he could now feel surrounding him. Even in the pitch darkness, he knew they were there. Huge and monstrous. Ogres, who wanted to be entertained by stories about themselves.

One of them, in what was not precisely a voice, said, 'Tell it.'

David laid his forehead on the cool compacted soil. 'Harry...'

Horrible sounds that may have been laughter. 'Want us to bring him here?'

'No! Please don't! Please!'

Ogre-ish laughter. 'Tell us.'

David tried to compose himself, to forget his son, his wife, his home, his life, to forget everything but the story, to call all the elements into place. If he told it well enough, perhaps they would let him live. Perhaps they would let him go home. But it was so difficult to concentrate. In the dark, his naked body caressed by hot, foul carrion breath, his mind saw only what it wanted to see, what it wanted to remember, and it wasn't the story.

He saw Harry taking his first feed from Louise's breast, and Louise's face shining up at David in maternal triumph. He saw the boy's first moments of toddling, his tears when he fell, the determination on his face as he climbed gamely back to his feet. He saw the gleam in Harry's blue eyes as David brought him another story like a perfect gift, one each night, until the night he accidentally brought a gift that was like a poisoned apple in a fairy tale.

David thought about his own father never telling him even one single story, and he wondered if his father had *known* that things like this could happen. He wondered if his father had known about the Hill People, or kinfolk of theirs in the place they had lived when David was a child.

He wondered if his father had known that there was both white *and* black to the Magic Hour, and that the white, however pure, could sometimes draw the black. If you were in the wrong place at the wrong time.

The Magic Hour was over.

Some time ago, I became interested in the idea of writing a dark fairytale for children, and this was the result. It starts off cutesy enough, but it steadily becomes darker and darker as it goes along until eventually it becomes something you might not want to read to a child around bedtime. Oh well, you win some, you lose some...

Before he even opened his eyes, he knew that something was wrong. He didn't know what it was, or why something should have gone wrong, he simply knew that it had. He opened his eyes and raised his forehead from his paws, blinking a little at the light as he looked about him.

Randolph Honey-Bunny was in the largest clearing in the forest that lay to the west of his home, which was the bank of an old dried up river now riddled with warrens. Despite the initial brightness he'd experienced when he'd first opened his eyes, he knew that the day was fading fast and twilight was nearly upon him, for the shadows thrown by the giant trees were longer and there was a distinct chill in the midsummer air. He was totally alone.

He sat up and raised his paws high above his head, until they brushed the tops of his ears, and he yawned sleepily. 'Now what,' he thought to himself, 'am I doing here?'

He wasn't too surprised when an answer didn't immediately occur to him, because when the truth was told, Randolph was the most forgetful rabbit anyone of his acquaintance could remember ever having met. And he was one of those truthful little rabbits who always told the truth and could never lie, not even to himself. Many times he had admitted aloud, "Randolph, you are the most stupid and forgetful - and the sleepiest - of all rabbits," and his Ma and Pa, for all their love of him, could only nod and smile ruefully.

With a little sigh, Randolph lay back down on a patch of moss and stretched out contentedly. He did his best thinking when he was completely horizontal, and sometimes it helped even more if he closed his eyes too. His mind always seemed to be racing with thoughts when he was in this comfortable position, but sooner or later − and more than likely sooner than later − he always fell into a doze that could last, if uninterrupted, the best part of a whole day.

'So,' he thought now, 'perhaps it would be better, just this once, *not* to close my eyes. It's almost night-time already and to sleep again might mean danger.' The forest could be a dangerous place for a rabbit at night, or so his Ma and Pa had always told him, and he had no reason to doubt their word.

Above Randolph's head the tree-tops swayed to and fro gently, and so high were they that they seemed to be painting the darkening sky with dirty rainclouds. The little rabbit watched for a while as the branches filled in the sky with black clouds, becoming gradually bolder and more adventurous in their movements until the clouds were huge monsters, swollen with rainwater, thunder and lightning, and angry with mayhem. 'Soon there will be a storm,' he told himself. 'Then I will have to run and find shelter until it passes. I will have to hide.'

And it was then that he remembered how it was he came to be in the clearing on his own in the first place.

He had been gambolling through the forest with all his brothers and sisters that afternoon when one of his brothers – he couldn't remember which – had suggested that they play a game of hide and seek, a game they had been taught by a drifting family of hares the week before.

Everyone had agreed to this, as they all enjoyed games, and after much argument it had been decided that Randolph was to be 'it'. So, after having had the rules of this new-ish game re-explained to him two or three times, Randolph had set about covering his eyes with his paws and counting to one hundred, or to the number of rabbits who made up the members of his immediate family – whichever came first.

Now, Randolph, who in addition to his other faults was not a great scholar, had agreed to this rule readily enough. But when all his brothers and sisters had disappeared from sight and he was alone with the task before him, it had suddenly dawned upon him that he didn't know the exact number of his family members - and he had never managed to count up to one hundred successfully in his entire life.

However, in the interests of not spoiling everyone's fun, he'd dutifully decided that he would at least try, and he'd replaced his paws over his eyes, leant against a tree and begun to count.

Three or four times he'd begun the strenuous mental trek toward this massive sum, and each time he'd had to start all over again, either because his attention had wandered or something had happened which irritated him, such as a fly landing on one of his enormous ears, making him forget where he was. Finally, he'd managed to get off to a good start, saying the numbers under his breath so that only he could hear them.

Randolph remembered reaching thirty. He remembered reaching forty, and he even remembered congratulating himself upon reaching fifty, but what happened after that was a total blank. And, of course, now it was obvious what had happened.

He had fallen asleep.

It was also equally obvious that his brothers and sisters must have eventually tired of hiding and gone home to the warren, assuming that he had done the same thing when he'd been unable to find them. Randolph giggled to himself, one more of his many habits. 'How they will all laugh when I tell them what really happened,' he thought.

Suddenly, from the distance, a wave of thunder rolled across the cloud-black sky and swept through the forest, accompanied by an icy whirlwind which whipped Randolph's ears about his head like a furry hat.

Randolph quickly stood up, eyeing the heavy clouds with a furrowed brow. 'This is not a storm to hide from under a tree,' he said quietly. 'This is a storm to hide from in the warren, in the warm, safe earth.' And so saying he set out for home, keeping one eye on the path ahead and the other on the dark clouds swirling high above.

Step by step, Randolph realised just how late the hour had become, and step by step he became more and more afraid – and not just because of the storm that threatened at any moment to fall to earth as though judgement day had come. In the days before he or his brothers and sisters had been allowed out on their own, they had been told terrible tales of darkness and mystery, not by Ma or Pa, but by the older rabbits who came to sit with them during the winter nights.

One very old rabbit in particular had been prone to telling them the most frightening stories, even though he had been asked not to by their parents. His name had been Humbert Baloney-Bunny, a tall-tale-telling traveller who had attached himself to them for a number of months before passing on to fresher fields and unsullied ears.

Randolph's memory of Humbert was very strong, but his memory of one of Humbert's tales was even stronger, for when he'd first heard it he'd been reduced to floods of tears and petrified with fear.

It was an age-old story of something called the Great Rabbit, an enormous, black, bestial rabbit which would sometimes materialise from thin air when the life of a very special rabbit was endangered.

Randolph, who had always privately thought of himself as something special, now realised that this story had been told to comfort, but at this present moment, while the world was in engulfed in a black storm and he was far from home, he felt less than comforted - and, in truth, less than special.

For if there were strange supernatural rabbits stalking the earth, what else might there be out there, hidden amongst the trees? Randolph shivered and refused to speculate further, but still his fears grew and grew.

Meanwhile, the pace of his steps steadily increased until he was almost running. He didn't dare attempt his greatest speed as the forest was now extremely dim, the light which had once dominated seemingly blown away by the gales which met him head on, pressing his ears down along the length of his back and flattening his whiskers across his cheeks. Just one false step at such a speed and he would probably race into a tree.

Another peal of thunder shook the trees to his left and right and he came to a gasping, shivering halt in a small clearing created by a newly fallen tree. Randolph cowered under a cluster of ferns bowed down by the wind. He was so frightened by the ferocity of the storm that he felt like crying, and he doubted that he even had the courage to move another inch, though he knew that he had to try.

Just as he was attempting to gather his nerve and his strength for another sprint, Randolph heard something that sounded uncommonly like a voice. He pricked up his ears. He stood stock still. He held his breath, and when the sound came again he knew for certain that he was not alone in the forest any more.

'Well, well, well,' the voice said. 'And what do we have here?'

Randolph swallowed nervously and then replied, 'Please, sir, I'm a rabbit.'

'Goodness gracious me,' the voice said with a low chuckle. 'A lonely rabbit, lost in the forest and running from the storm. Tell me, little one, how did you happen to be here so late in the day, and without your little family?'

'Please, sir,' Randolph answered politely, as his Ma and Pa had always taught him. 'I was playing a game called hide and seek with my brothers and sisters, and I... Well, sir, I think I fell asleep...'

'You fell asleep?' the voice inquired and then broke up into deep, hearty laughter.

'Yes, sir, but I'm not lost at all, I know exactly where I am. My burrow lies to the east, sir, and I could reach it within half an hour were it not for the storm.'

'To the east you say?' the voice asked, its laughter becoming deeper still. 'Interesting. Very interesting.'

There was a sudden noise of rapid movement which had Randolph peering into the darkness, trying to catch a glimpse of this confident, jolly sounding stranger, but all he could see were outlines. Outlines of the ferns he was sheltering under, outlines of the fallen tree and its splintered stump, and outlines of the trees beyond.

And then, without him even having to lie down and close his eyes, a thought sprang into his mind as if by magic.

'Please, sir,' he said.

'Yes?' answered the voice through its laughter.

'Please, sir, am I special?'

'Special? Why of course you are!'

Randolph beamed to himself with pleasure. 'Then you must be the Great Rabbit, come to save me from the storm.'

There was a brief moment of silence before the mysterious voice spoke again. When it did, there was no laughter left in it. Not one jot. 'And who, pray tell, is the 'Great Rabbit'?'

Randolph should have been warned by this question and the way in which it was asked, but somehow he was not. The very idea that he really was special had driven his common sense away, and the words bubbled out from his tiny lips as though he had made his tongue a miser and saved up all his words for a month.

'Please, sir,' he said rapidly, 'the Great Rabbit is a giant, magical rabbit that jumps up from nowhere whenever a special rabbit is in danger. It saves the special rabbits and guides them safely home, and it punishes those who have threatened them, and nothing on earth can stop it once it has appeared.'

There was another ominous silence.

'I see,' the voice said at length, so quietly that Randolph had to strain to hear the words. 'In that case, I'm sorry to have misled you.'

'Misled me, sir? How have you misled me?'

The voice chuckled again, but there was more satisfaction in the laughter than there was genuine humour. 'It seems that you are *not* a special rabbit after all,' it said. 'Merely an unfortunate one. You see, you will never see your home ever again...'

At that moment, even as Randolph was listening nervously to these awful words, the storm suddenly broke and a long sequence of lightning bolts split the sky, illuminating the whole of the forest with an eerie blue light. Randolph's wish to see the stranger was now fulfilled, and he wished that it had not. There, six yards ahead of him, blocking his path home, was a large red fox, his fur bristling and his sharp teeth bared.

'As you can now see,' the fox said in a loud voice, shaking his head slightly as the first of the raindrops hit his nose, 'I am not your Great Rabbit. I am Tibor the Fox, and the only special thing about you is that you will be the last thing I shall eat before I sleep this evening.'

Without waiting for another word, Randolph turned his white tail toward the fox and ran into the bracken as fast as he could. There was no sense now in blaming himself for giving away his destination so glibly. Likewise, there was no use now in worrying about running into trees, for he needed all his speed to escape the terrible danger which was racing after him. To hit a tree and be knocked unconscious would be far better than being caught by vicious stages, dragged down by the ankles by an enemy as ruthless as Tibor the Fox.

Tales of the cruel Tibor were as common as they were of the Great Rabbit, but the Great Rabbit, Randolph now realised, was only a tale and no more, while Tibor was a dangerous reality.

'Run,' he told himself. 'Run until you can run no more!'

Randolph accelerated to his maximum speed, forcing himself beyond his own endurance until he could only see his paws as a grey blur in the general darkness. He swerved around trees, dodging under and over their roots, and he ploughed through thick seas of bracken, twisting and turning, constantly slipping on the rain-wet undergrowth, as he hoped to confuse his pursuer.

But Tibor the Fox was not a creature to be lost so easily.

For seven long years had Tibor lived and hunted in this forest, and for two years before that in other parts of the surrounding countryside, and in all that time he had captured and eaten many hundreds of rabbits. It had been a few good years indeed since any rabbit he had set his heart on eating had escaped him.

Tibor knew all their tricks, all their hiding places, and he knew that he would sleep deeply that night, with a full belly and the sweet taste of a young buck rabbit lingering in his mouth.

By this time, confused by the darkness and the heavy rain, Randolph had ceased to run in any particular direction and the only thought that occupied his frightened mind was flight. He could hear Tibor fighting his way through the bracken, close behind most of the time, with only the occasional moment where he could not feel the presence of the fox's eyes and smell the hungry breath from the fox's mouth.

At first, Randolph had thought that he was beginning to leave Tibor behind, but as the terrible sequence was repeated over and over again - the fox disappearing and then returning ever closer - he realised that he was being shepherded, against his will, to some place chosen by his pursuer. Some place, more than likely, where there was no cover, no bolt hole, and where the end would be sudden and painful.

As this last thought crossed his mind, Randolph burst through the lower branches of a small bush and abruptly found himself with no earth under his flailing paws. He was flying through the air, his body twisting, and he was conscious of a stinging sensation in his right ear. The earth quickly rushed up to meet him, knocking all the remaining breath from his panting body, and then he was rolling uncontrollably along a shallow furrow, his head meeting stones and rocks, his claws grasping as he desperately sought to bring himself to a halt. Finally, he lay still, winded, bruised and begrimed with dirt and blood. Randolph painfully sat up and looked around, and then back the way he had come.

The little rabbit was in a large flat field, recently ploughed and now left fallow, and behind him stood a barbed wire fence, the three lengths of wire seemingly holding back the thick forest from trespassing into the sanctity of the field. On one of the barbs Randolph could see a tuft of his own fur and a drop of blood running along the wire from the point where it had caught his ear. A desperate hope surged into his mind. 'Perhaps the barbed wire will hold back the fox, perhaps I will be saved after all.'

But the chill answer came in the form of a shrill fox's bark and the terrible sight of Tibor the Fox leaping out of the depths of the forest, clearing the fence with ease.

Randolph turned to run again, but in his heart of hearts he knew that he couldn't go on. The chase through the forest had left him exhausted and the fall into the field had driven all the fight out of him. But, as always, he made the effort and bravely ran on, his pace now no greater than a slow walk, and at his very side Tibor the Fox trotted easily as he quickly regained his own breath.

'Very good, little one,' the fox said as they approached the centre of the field. 'You were very fast, and you are very brave, but this is where it ends.'

Finally, unable to take even one more step, Randolph sank down on to the ground and lay there breathing heavily. He was so tired that he hardly even noticed the rain pounding on his body. 'At least, sir,' he managed to gasp, his hot breath becoming visible in the cold night air. 'At least I made you work for your meal, even though I am not special.'

The fox walked stiff-legged toward his quarry and stopped when his head was directly over Randolph's inert body. Only then did he speak. 'Indeed you did, little one,' Tibor said, allowing a drop of saliva to slip off his tongue and fall on to the rabbit's back, making him tremble. 'Indeed you did, but my work is done now - and I must have my prize.'

Randolph closed his eyes just as tightly as he could, imagining at any moment that the fox's jaws would clamp around his neck and shake and shake and shake. But the fox's jaws didn't touch him. Nothing touched him. Instead, he heard a noise which was strangely familiar.

It took Randolph only a moment to recognise this unexpected sound, and when he did his heart was cheered. It was the sound of rabbits' feet pounding the earth. A multitude of rabbits coming closer, travelling at speed. Warily, but with a growing hope, he opened his eyes and saw Tibor the Fox staring thoughtfully into the distance. Randolph followed the fox's line of vision and saw hundreds of rabbits running toward them.

Tibor the Fox licked his lips delightedly. 'Your friends have come to help you, little one,' he laughed. 'This will be no meal, little one, this will be a *feast*!'

But Randolph Honey-Bunny had seen something that the fox with his supreme confidence had not. In addition to the rabbits which Tibor had already spotted, equal numbers were heading for them from the other three corners of the field, and they were far from being Randolph's friends, for he had never seen their like before.

They were black rabbits.

Each and every one, from the first to the thousandth, was completely black.

'Better look behind you, Mr Fox,' Randolph said quietly, an uneasy feeling coming over him as the black rabbits came closer and closer, racing over the fallow field toward them. 'Better take care, Tibor,' he said. 'These rabbits are not like me. You cannot eat these rabbits.'

Tibor the Fox sneered. 'I can eat any rabbit in the world,' he boasted, and then out of the corner of his eye he caught sight of the rest of the rabbits who were now very close indeed. The fox began to turn around rapidly, spinning around and around, suddenly wary and on his guard. 'What is this?' he demanded of Randolph angrily. 'What does this mean?'

But Randolph had no answers to offer, for he was just as mystified as the fox himself. All he could say, in a tiny voice trembling with apprehension, was, 'Look!'

Tibor the Fox looked, and a combined expression of panic and fear took over his narrow face, transforming it from the face of a born killer into the face of a creature in absolute terror.

Twenty feet away from him, the entire horde of black rabbits had chosen to make their stand in one colossal pack. They stood and snarled at the fox, and it chilled him to the bone to see that their teeth, razor sharp though they were, were as black as their skins.

As far as Tibor the Fox was concerned, these creatures were not rabbits. They were unnatural beasts spewed up from some unholy pit deep in the earth, and what he saw next through eyes wide with fear convinced him doubly that he was right.

Before him, the black rabbits began to leap up and cling to their fellows' backs, and then without a pause other rabbits were following after, until small columns were formed which then joined with other columns to form a concentrated black mass.

Frozen with fear, Tibor watched the process of this incredible spectacle with no idea of what it might mean, but he was filled all the while with a deep foreboding. Second by second the black mountain of rabbits grew more immense, their separate bodies melting together, becoming indistinguishable from each other in the darkness, until they became... *one*.

The fox suddenly gave a sharp yelp, a scream, as he realised what Randolph, still laid in the mud close to unconsciousness, had already realised. The enormous black mound which had been a thousand rabbits was slowly defining itself into a certain shape, no less incredible just because it was so familiar.

The tale was not merely a tale, the myth not merely a myth. It was a fearsome reality.

Towering above Tibor the Fox was the Great Rabbit.

Tibor turned immediately and tried to run, but the Great Rabbit raised its gigantic paw and lashed out, catching the terrified fox on his side and sending him flying across the field where he rolled and clattered and eventually ended in a red, furry heap, sodden with mud and rain and blood, his entire side torn open.

Too amazed to do anything except watch, Randolph lay still as the badly injured fox slowly raised himself on shaking legs, took one long last look at the Great Rabbit and then ran away as quickly as he could, tripping over his own paws in his haste and leaving a blood trail that was vivid on the dark earth for a few moments before the rain washed it away.

Randolph's brain was reeling, and he could feel himself losing consciousness. The fox had caught him, and he had been as good as dead, but he was *not* dead. The Great Rabbit had saved him – but saved him for what? Did he, in the end, fear the Great Rabbit more than he did the fox?

Finally, it was all too much for the little rabbit and his eyes closed of their own accord. The world became completely black, and peaceful, and the last thing that he saw before he passed out was a red tail, tucked firmly between a pair of red legs, as it disappeared into the forest.

Randolph was safe now, comfortably curled up between his slumbering brothers and sisters in the very deepest burrow in the entire warren. 'Brothers to the left, sisters to the right,' he thought. 'The cosiest bed anyone ever had.' A short distance away, Ma and Pa were also asleep, and he promised himself that he would pray for them both extra hard before he went to sleep.

It had been Ma and Pa, who had been searching for him half the night, who had eventually found him in the muddy field in the early hours of the morning, still unconscious and half frozen, and brought him home. He'd been sternly told off, of course, as they'd cleaned him up and taken care of his wounded ear, and his brothers and sisters had been told off, too, for leaving him in the forest in the first place. But none of that mattered now that he was safe. Neither of them were really angry.

Randolph himself was very happy despite his hardships, though he was surprised that he hadn't already joined the rest of the rabbits in their restful sleep. After all, he was still exhausted from his adventure, and the other conditions were just right - his body was horizontal and his eyes were closed.

'Why aren't I asleep?' he asked himself. But as he asked himself this question, he realised that he already knew the answer.

In the warm darkness of the burrow, Randolph grinned to himself. What a day he'd had! In one day he'd had three experiences that a thousand rabbits could live a thousand lifetimes and never have.

In a fallow field, on the brink of death, he'd seen the great and terrible Tibor the Fox being taught a lesson he would never forget. In a fallow field, he had seen the Great Rabbit do the teaching. And in a fallow field, he had finally known the truth about himself.

He was a special rabbit, after all.

Come Back is the short story that was the inspiration for the full-length novel Comeback, *a small excerpt of which ends this collection. Oddly enough, even though it was the thematic starting point for the novel, not one word of the short story was ever written down until months after the novel itself was finished. It just lived in my mind, unchanged, until its time to be written came around.*

He found the teeth first.

Staggering out of his pit, half-blind with sleep, the Saturday morning hangover like a curse. Across the dark, cluttered bedroom, out through the hall, into the chilly, too-bright bathroom, so weak he had to sit down on the toilet to piss. Elbows on his knees, both hands pressed to his temples trying to hold his splitting head together. *Shit*. How much had he had to drink last night? He discovered he had no memory after around nine o'clock. Double *shit*. The piss burned as it passed out of him, which was never a good sign, and he could feel his poor head trying to burst open like a seed pod. What had he been drinking by the *end* of the night?

Only then did the nagging pain on the sole of his foot register, finally, on his poor shrivelled brain. Then he noticed the irregular crimson smears padding across the bathroom tiles. When he bent further over and raised his leg to look for the epicentre of the pain, he saw an even semi-circle of red indentations spread across the ball of his left foot, tiny wells of dark, oily-looking blood, like teeth marks. Like someone had bitten him.

Teeth marks? Really?

After splashing his face with frigid tap-water and swallowing three or four aspirin, he hesitated in his bedroom doorway. He vaguely remembered catching his foot on something as he wove his way across the darkened room, but the strain on his bladder had seemed much more important at the time. Now he was curious, but with his thick, lined curtains obliterating the single window the room was as black as the Guinness he'd started the evening on last night. Even with the benefit of the daylight from the hallway behind him and the door wide open he could still see virtually nothing. He was suddenly unable to shake the idea that someone was either asleep or unconscious on his bedroom floor and he'd managed to stamp on their face on the way to the bathroom.

He leaned in, turned on the overhead light, and revealed the mild chaos of his bachelor's life.

Glossy magazines, stiff tissues, a week or more's backlog of dirty clothes, mugs, plates, newspapers, pizza boxes, and junk mail, all scattered over the floor around his messy bed like bones around a predator's lair. But happily no surprise overnight visitor rolled up in his guest sleeping bag nursing a freshly broken jaw. This was quite a relief, actually, if for no other reason than the fact that some of his glossies were kind of specialist publications, and definitely not to everyone's taste.

He had just begun to relax again when the itching discomfort on his right sole reminded him that the morally questionable nature of his porn wasn't really the point here. The question was, what had he caught himself on that was sharp enough to make him bleed? Because he *knew* it couldn't have been what it looked like from the bloody holes in his foot. That would make no sense at all.

He carefully waded into the debris of his bachelor life, carefully nudging the layers of crap aside with his toes, until, only two minutes later, he found the teeth. The upper plate of a set of incredibly ancient dentures, in fact, the plate the colour of over-stewed tea and the pegs themselves the diseased ivory of ancient urinals.

So his wound was exactly what it looked like, after all.

His fresh blood gave the discoloured teeth's unlikely sharp edges a jolly pink trim, and he began to wonder if he might need a tetanus shot or something.

Saturday afternoon. Late, late breakfast in a greasy spoon, picking out winners in the paper and backing losers down the bookies. A frame of snooker down the social club with his ex's dad, then a couple of cheeky solo pints in The Cock while watching the final scores come in on the TV behind the bar. He dawdled on the way home. Bought a couple of cheap DVDs while picking up a six-pack at the supermarket, then hit the local pizza house for takeout. Headed home again for a restful night in. Blow-out, piss-up, Match of the Day, action fest'. Lovely. And Sunday still to come.

It was nearly eight by the time he let himself back into his one-bedroom flat on the thirteenth floor. He knew he'd been out for a lot longer than usual, walking slower and slower and letting his food go cold and his beer go warm, but he hadn't realised why. He did now. The smell hit him like a slap around the face and he dropped his shopping without even knowing he'd done it. Smelled like something gone real bad, or even something burning, maybe.

He went through the flat, turning on lights as he went, trying not to panic. Left a ciggie burning, he thought, Christ...

After only a few moments he was forced to accept that nothing was burning, but fuck, *something* stank to high heaven. He went back to close the front door, then scraped up his fractured pizza on to a plate, stuck it and the booze in the fridge, tossed the DVDs on to the counter. Where was the smell worst, he asked himself? There was no question about it, it was far worse in the living room.

As he started gingerly sniffing around, trying to locate the source of the stench, he saw the dentures he'd placed on the mantle above the old gas fire, like a mock trophy. They looked like they were grinning at him.

He went down on all fours to sniff behind and underneath the furniture, and eventually ended up at the cabinet where he kept his private DVD collection, the ones he didn't want anyone else seeing. The sliding door of the cheap little unit was stuck open half an inch, as usual. He stuck his nose into the aperture and sniffed, and then recoiled as though something had bitten it. The other half of the set of teeth?

Angry now, as if the whole thing was a practical joke that had outlasted whatever desperate humour it might once have held, he violently slid the door the rest of the way open. A battered men's lace-up shoe tumbled out of the cabinet and lay on its side between his knees.

There was a foot in the shoe.

When he came back from flushing his breakfast, he found he was trembling. He studied the foot without actually touching it. It was real, no kind of joke, practical or otherwise. It had unhealthy yellow skin, and was almost hairless. It wore a fuzzy brown woollen sock that had ridden down under the heel. There was far too much detail for it to be a joke. It was too fucking *awful* to be anybody's idea of a joke.

There were about three inches of leg left above the ankle, and two bones stuck up another inch or so out of the severed end. Where the flesh had been cut, the skin was puckered tight, the meat between it and the bones grey-black, as though it had been frozen. Up close the smell of it made his eyes water.

He picked up the shoe by the sole and the worn heel, careful not to touch the rubbery, infected-looking flesh above, and placed it on the mantle beside the teeth. He took two or three steps back, and then decided that this really wasn't far enough to get the thing in perspective. He backed all the way to the kitchen, where he remembered that he had new booze in the fridge. A drink seemed like a very good idea. Steady his nerves.

He fumbled at the fridge door and then at a ring pull. He drank, hissed at the bite, and felt better. But then didn't.

Suddenly the bad smell seemed much stronger again – but this time in the kitchen.

He opened his eyes. He was sitting on the living room floor, his back against the sofa, facing the TV. On the screen somebody was going wild with a machine gun. Action fest'. On the floor to his right were five empty and crushed beer cans and a sixth one that was as yet unopened. Piss-up. To his left was his cold, broken pizza, not a single bite taken out of it that he could see. The blow-out hadn't happened, his stomach obviously wasn't ready for food. On the TV, people were screaming, automatic weapons were hammering. The smell now clung to his clothes like the smoke from a bonfire.

He was drunk once more and felt like vomiting again.

Go on, look.

No, it won't be there.

He looked, and it was. Up on the mantle, on the other side of the teeth to the foot, was a mousy brown toupee, encrusted with thick black mud and crawling with lice. And not just a toupee alone - the false hair was stuck to a *real* scalp, complete with ears. A kind of clear liquid was oozing out of the flesh, and it had run down the front of the mantle like treacle. He'd found the hair in the cupboard under the sink. How long ago now, he didn't know.

He opened the last can of beer quickly, managed a huge double-swallow before it all came up again, plus interest. He twisted to his side and emptied what was left of his stomach contents over the pizza.

He opened his eyes. He was slumped in the hallway outside the living room, and he could hear somebody fucking. Very, very drunk now, a half-empty whisky bottle by his side, the last of the emergency booze. Fucking?

He let his heavy head roll along the wall until he faced the doorway to the living room. The back of the armchair blocked out most of the TV screen, but he could make out the shapes of two men and a woman going for it. He knew this DVD well. The scene was about halfway through. He had no memory of starting it.

Very drunk. Could hardly see straight, let alone move. The severed arm he had discovered down the back of the sofa lay near the fireplace where he'd dropped it in disgust. He could still feel the rotting looseness of the skin on the palms of his hands, and they were itching badly. A part of the arm and the crude-looking hand at the end of it was visible around the side of the armchair.

He blinked and tried to focus on it. Could he really see the fingers twitching?

He closed his eyes. The smell became worse. There was a sound. He opened his eyes again. Saw.

Oh. My. *God.*

It came rocking out from behind the armchair. The torso.

No arms, no legs, naked. It had a head, but it didn't have a face, just a glistening mask of muscles and tendons. No eyes. No nose, just a beak of gristle. Rocking, rocking, rocking, chest and stomach muscles working, head swaying forwards and backwards, as though it were humping the carpet. Toothless mouth open, wetly gasping, like it was echoing the sounds the woman on the TV was making.

A little groan was forced out with each undulation. Each groan seemed a little more triumphant than the one that preceded it, he thought. Why? Because it was reaching its goal, obviously. It stopped when its flayed cranium hit the sofa, and then blindly buried its non-face in his abandoned pizza, slobbering up his puke along with the more orthodox toppings.

Why not? It was all nourishment.

He opened his eyes. He was lying on his side on the bed in his darkened bedroom, the big overhead light from the hallway spilling in. Comfy cosy. Then the slick arm around his neck tightened its grip, and a cold wet body shifted against his back, and a sticky toothless voice smacked into his ear:

'Find my eyes...'

He woke up on the sofa feeling as though someone had stuck a spade in his head. It was almost dawn, and he could hear a few early birds starting to sing. Sunday morning. It was standing at his side, naked, grinning down at him, and he closed his eyes again.

Prayed a little.

Opened them.

'Still here,' it said.

He only dimly remembered stumbling through his flat with it clinging to his back. For hours, it'd felt like. Looking through cupboards, behind furniture, in jars and boxes, searching for all its missing bits and pieces. Finding them.

The only find he remembered with any clarity was the first, the eyes. Fished out of the rancid oil of the chip-pan he'd stuck away in the oven more than a month before, the last time he'd cooked anything resembling a meal. He'd passed the eyes over his shoulder one by one, each greeted with a hoot of triumph and then a squelching, sucking sound that reminded him once again of one of his porn DVDs. He felt sure that he had passed out, probably more than once, in the pursuit of its legs and remaining arm.

Now it stood complete beside him. It was about six foot three and looked like the sort of man anyone with any sense would avoid, even under normal circumstances. These were not normal circumstances.

He could see the points at which its limbs had been reattached, great swollen bands of discolouration like scar tissue. Its thick twisted cock was almost black, its heavy balls hanging down to mid-thigh level, bristling with coarse grey hairs.

'Like what you see?'

He couldn't say no, couldn't even shake his head, and of course it knew this. The face, lined with deep wrinkles, didn't appear to have been put back on entirely straight, but when it smiled its awful dentures were fully revealed, so everything was working.

He tracked it with his eyes as it turned away. It began to pull items of clothing from the armchair, dressing awkwardly, still uncertain of its balance. First its missing sock, then a pair of ragged y-fronts, the crotch like leopard skin, pissy-yellow and spotted with black mould like the stuff on the kitchen ceiling. The pants to a threadbare grey linen suit, a shirt with a stud collar, a wide 40s-style tie, and the jacket to the suit. He winced when it slammed its foot into the second shoe.

Finally, it pulled on a mud-streaked black overcoat with a long tear in the right sleeve, edged with dried blood. It turned back and reached for him and he shrank away, a scream trapped at the back of his throat. Then he saw that it was holding out its hand to him. To be shaken.

Reluctantly, he took it, felt his own hand enclosed and gripped too hard for comfort. He saw a network of old deep scars scoring the inside of its wrist, and shuddered.

'Thank you,' it said.

It turned to leave the room, but then paused. The sense of relief, of unlikely escape, that he'd begun to feel flooded away immediately. It turned back, looked at him, then glanced around the rest of the room, its eyes settling on the armchair, considering. Then it stepped back, reached down the side of the cushion and plucked out a battered fedora with a bullet hole burned through the brim.

'Can't go out without a hat,' it said. 'See you again, soon.'

Ten minutes after it had gone, he finally managed to get up from the sofa. He shuffled over to the window like an arthritic old man and opened it wide, leaning out, breathing deeply.

No one saw him jump, and he didn't scream on the way down.

Despite the subject of this story, I don't personally believe that violent movies and video games drive people to commit murder. Violence, after all, has been Mankind's favourite hobby since the dawn of time. And if a mass murderer or serial killer is looking for inspiration, they're as likely to find it in Grimm's faery tales or the TV guide as anywhere else. Or, if all else fails, I suppose they can always claim that their dog told them to do it....

Yoshimitzu arrives in disguise as a creature of the night. He has found a long black overcoat that reaches down almost to his cleated boots, and he has turned the wide collar up so that it cradles his head like a bowl. He has whitened his face with powder, darkened and gelled his hair into a forest of spikes, and shadowed and lined his eyes with the artistry of a geisha. The shopping mall's lights gleam on his wraparound sunglasses like moonlight on a dark, becalmed ocean. Beneath the surface, a leviathan silently cruises, emanating threat and the promise of destruction.

He strolls alone past the closed boutiques and department stores, a legion of mannequin eyes following his mannered progress with mute approval, and then turns toward the short queue he can see has formed at the entrance to the subterranean nightclub. This is his destination.

This is his destiny.

The two men on the door are identical twins, and also joint owners of the nightclub, and they alone select those who may enter the exclusivity of their domain and those who may not. As he slows his pace to join the back of the queue, Yoshimitzu sees two young men in football shirts turned away, and then another man who is clearly deemed to be too old, too normal, is turned away also, all of them absently redirected to establishments more suitable to their particular niches.

The couple in front of him will have no such trouble gaining entrance. The male is dressed much as Yoshimitzu is, although his hair has been bleached as white as bone, and the female wears a tiny black skirt, not much wider than the studded belt above it, and fishnet stockings that she has deliberately ripped in provocative places. Yoshimitzu can see bruises on the outsides of her thighs, and high on the inside of the left, a large suck-mark she seems proud to display. When she briefly turns to clock him, he sees that beneath her leather jacket she wears a filmy lace halter top which only just manages to contain her large creamy white breasts.

Yoshimitzu smiles. The female smiles back. He is in disguise, and so is she. Everyone is in disguise.

But some disguises are better than others.

When it is his turn to be scrutinised, Yoshimitzu sails through the doorway without attracting comment. The twins are still smiling together over the girl in the fishnets, and they wave him through automatically, and then turn their attention to a large group of newcomers. His disguise has successfully made him invisible.

Yoshimitzu follows the couple down the tight spiral staircase into the basement nightclub, and the music that was only a dull, repetitive thud at the doorway quickly becomes a thunder of industrial percussion, with a pulsing undercurrent of throbbing bass. Distorted electric guitars like sheets of broken glass slice through the air around him, and it sounds like a call to battle.

The nightclub is very full, although it is not as large as it initially appears. The walls have been mirrored floor to ceiling, creating the illusion, all the people sitting at the small tables set around the edge of the dance floor doubled, and then doubled again, and then again. The crowd at the long bar that takes up a whole wall is four and five deep, arms held aloft, banknotes in their hands, clamouring for the bar staff's attention. They too are doubled and redoubled in the mirrored bar, until they resemble a standing army saluting Yoshimitzu, their champion.

The dance floor is crowded, hectic with lights. A new song begins, indistinguishable from the last, but it is greeted by the nightclub's customers like an old favourite, a beat like the commanding drum in a Roman galley, a whining voice even more penetrating and abrasive than the guitars. More people surge on to the dance floor in response. Some shuffle to the music. Some jump. Some thrash. Some push. Some stomp.

Yoshimitzu begins to ease his way through the knots and clumps of people. On the edge of the dance floor, two young women seated on stools ostentatiously kiss under a fixed spotlight, tonguing each other deeply, feeding on the attention as vampires feed on blood. Yoshimitzu carefully negotiates his way to the very centre of the dance floor, closes his eyes, and begins to meditate.

He puts everything else out of his mind. His mother, her sorrow, and her hidden bottles. His sister, and her poisonous, abusive boyfriend. The tiny room which had been his since he was a baby. The smell of mildew, and musty clothes, and blocked drains. The disappointments of his education, and the misery of zero-hours employment. None of it matters anymore.

He is here now, centred and calm in the moment. It is here that all his many lonely hours of training in his room finally bear fruit.

And so it begins…

With his eyes still closed, he slowly unbuttons the long coat and then shrugs it off his shoulders, lets it pile in a heap at his heels. He opens his eyes. No one is even looking at him. No one has seen the sheathed samurai sword hanging down his back.

Yoshimitzu reaches over his shoulder with his right hand and withdraws the sword from its sheath, then carefully settles both hands on the long haft as he raises it. Still, no one appears to have noticed.

Coloured messages flash in front of Yoshimitzu's eyes:

PLAYER SELECT

He selects. Then:

READY?

He is ready. And then:

FIGHT!

Yoshimitzu steps forward and deliberately kicks the man in front of him in the butt. When the man whirls about in anger, Yoshimitzu runs him through, the sword entering his chest as easily as Yoshimitzu himself had entered the nightclub, and for a second or two, he can feel the man's heart beating against his blade.

He pulls free, turns and pivots, and sidekicks a girl in the belly, and she flies away, knocking over a table and scattering the people sitting at it. The man the girl has been dancing with points at him, and Yoshimitzu chops off the accusing hand in a trice.

The screaming begins.

Yoshimitzu spins and back-kicks a tall man in the face, breaking his nose. The tall man is only held on his feet by the close-packed bodies of the other dancers who surround him, most of whom have not heard or understood the screams, and Yoshimitzu drops to one knee before him, slicing downward at the same time. The man's stomach opens up like a flower and his guts splatter out on to the dance floor.

Yoshimitzu rises once more, savagely elated, although his enemies still massively outnumber him. He feels that there is a real nobility to the combatants' deaths, and a strange cyclical energy at work. One enemy is defeated, and then is immediately reborn in another body, and the contest begins anew.

A girl slips in the tall man's guts and almost falls, and she looks down and sees the slippery coils of silver-purple intestine under her feet. When she bends over to spray vomit on her shoes, Yoshimitzu slices her head off in one swift, decisive blow, and blood erupts from her neck in an astonishing scarlet flood.

The music stops. There is shouting, screaming. People push, pull, try to run, get jammed together, trip, fall, clamber to their feet again, push, pull, try to run, get jammed, trip, fall....

Yoshimitzu sails in, swinging, hacking, thrusting.

He splits a man's head in two, opens the back of another down to the spine. He skewers one of the lipstick lesbians who were seated by the edge of the dance floor through the shoulder, then through her right thigh, then through her upraised palm as she begs him for mercy, and finally through her open, screaming mouth.

People are fighting each other, blindly panicking in their haste to climb the spiral staircase and escape. Others, with cooler heads, have hit the emergency exit and a flood of cooler air from the outside world flows inside. Peering down the staircase, holding steady against the flood of escapees, the twin owners are staring at him, one with a mobile phone clamped to his ear.

Yoshimitzu suddenly receives a blow to the back of his head, and he immediately spins and lashes out with his foot, but kicks nothing but air. He regains his balance and marks his new opponent. It is the bleached-haired man from the queue, and he is brandishing one of the bar stools at Yoshimitzu, threatening to use it like a club. Yoshimitzu feints at his head, and when the other man raises the heavy stool to counter the attack, Yoshimitzu spins on the spot, whirling around and around, swinging his sword out like the blade of a helicopter.

The stool tumbles heavily to the floor, and the man is backing away, one hand clamped to his arm, trying to stem the jets of blood from several long, deep cuts. *Please*, he says, *no, don't, please*. Yoshimitzu hacks him to pieces in a matter of seconds, and then turns, looking for his partner, the girl with the fishnet stockings and the creamy breasts, but she is nowhere to be seen.

While he has been finishing off the bleach-blond, the nightclub has mostly emptied, the last of the combatants having fled the arena, defeated and afraid. Their dead sprites litter the dance floor which is awash with blood and severed limbs. From the far distance there comes the sound of sirens, the sound of many sirens.

It is time to regroup, time to rebuild his strength.

Yoshimitzu gracefully lowers himself to the floor and sits cross-legged among the debris of his victory. He pumps his sword a few times, the blade only inches from his nose, recharging his energy levels.

Then he just sits and meditates, open to the world in anticipation of glory, and he smiles, and he thinks:

YOSHIMITZU WINS!

(Excerpt)

This is a very brief taste of Comeback, my first ever published horror novel, which is about Sam Parker, a writer whose fictional city, the hellish City of Eldritch, and some of its more fearsome citizens, are beginning to make bloody inroads into the real world.

Far sooner than he had ever expected, Sam found himself in his attic office with the night pressing at the windows like a giant moth. He was a little chilly even though he'd exchanged his wet clothes for dry ones, but like everything else the chill didn't register in his mind, because his mind was already full to bursting.

Sam blinked and he was sitting before his computer, which had been fired up. He had no memory of moving there, or of turning on the power.

He opened a new file with the format he always used for his novels. It was time to be honest, he thought. When you were looking at a blank screen that was the only thing to be if you wanted to write something worthwhile. He had told the audience at the convention that he'd just taken a holiday from

Eldritch. That's what he'd told everyone, including his agent and his friends.

But really, it was more like he'd run away from the city.

For some reason he didn't understand, the idea of writing the thirteenth Eldritch novel had begun to fill Sam with absolute dread the very moment he had finished the twelfth. The more so because he knew exactly what it would be about, what it *had* to be about. It had a pre-ordained quality he didn't like, but couldn't trust himself to resist.

Hence the distraction of the *Deep Water* novel. By looking at unfamiliar skies he had felt that he was striking a blow for self-preservation, and it had worked for a while. But holidays end, and someday everyone has to come home. As Sam was home now. He was wary of his fear and apprehension, but he still wanted to write the book. He wasn't sure he even had a choice.

One of his office walls was dominated by a large, framed Eldritch promotional poster. In heavy Gothic type against a blood-red background, it featured the three-word epigram that prefaced every Eldritch novel, and which had given the Eldritch fan club its name.

Stories Never End.

Sam had always believed that. He believed it now.

Unconsciously, he had allowed his hands to creep into the home position on his keyboard, and now he consciously pulled them back. Intellectually, he knew that he couldn't start this book. He hadn't planned anything. He had no synopsis, no outline, no notes. But tonight his intellect was asleep and his gut feeling was in control, and this told him that the story would write itself.

Even the title was a foregone conclusion, referring as it did not only to the ultimate ambition of the book's protagonist, a former Eldritch crime-boss who was dead and didn't want to be, but also to Sam's own return to the city.

No plan, no synopsis, no outline, but Sam knew exactly how it would begin, and where. Still filled with that strange combination of fear and excitement, he let his hands go back where they wanted to be. The keyboard, like his house, felt like home.

It was time to tell the world what really haunted Sly Jack Road.

He began to type...

10

COMEBACK
Part One
THE BEGINNING

CHAPTER ONE

Smooth Harry Flanagan, talented seducer of Eldritch's young women, had parked under the trees less than ten minutes ago with a pretty little seventeen-year-old called Rena White. Rena was a bright girl who knew her own mind, or thought she did. "Take me somewhere spooky, Harry," she'd demanded, so he'd driven her to the spookiest place he knew, Sly Jack Road.

Smooth Harry had opened the windows and lit Rena a cigarette even though he didn't smoke himself, because he was smooth enough to realise how sophisticated the cigarette made Rena feel. She was bright but she was still young enough to deceive herself that easily.

Perhaps it was thinking of her as a child that encouraged Smooth Harry, more than twenty years her senior, to tell Rena a few stories about dirty old Sly Jack Road. About the number of bodies reputed to have been buried here over the years, in shallow graves, and about the unquiet spirits that walked here after dark.

Tonight the night was dark indeed, and at this hour very few cars passed along the country lane. Even if there had been a traffic jam, however, the cars' occupants would not have seen Smooth Harry's ride. The old Honda Accord was black, and Smooth Harry had parked it deep under cover of the trees on the eastern side of the road. It was a good spot for intimacies, explorations, and fledgling understandings. He had used it before.

The ghost stories were going down very well, which was precisely what Smooth Harry was hoping young Rena would do after he'd loosened her up a little. Rena had lovely white skin, and when aroused or excited her face and arms turned bright pink, as though she'd just stepped out of a hot bath. Smooth Harry was desperate to see if the rest of her body reacted the same way.

Rena was staring at him with those big, big eyes as he spoke and the cool night air slipped into the car through the open windows. Without interrupting the flow of the story he was telling her - and making up as he went along, as it happened - Smooth Harry casually leaned across to take off Rena's safety belt. As he eased the belt across, he let the back of his hand graze over her breasts and felt that her nipples were already hard, like little knuckles under her blouse. Her colour rose and her eyes seemed to shimmer and dilate at his touch, but Smooth Harry never let on that he had noticed, because that wouldn't have been smooth.

He wanted to be so careful, so gentle with this one. He was gentle with most of his conquests, those who needed it to be gentle, but this one was special. He didn't understand why, but this one was very special.

Smooth Harry's mouth, spinning tales, seemed to be working independently of his brain, which was making up its own story. He imagined Rena's mini-skirt rucked up high around her waist, little black panties twisted into a glistening cord dividing her labia, her white thighs spread wide and burning like radiators. So gentle. Her sweet succulence oiling his fingers. The provocation of her nipples to bite, bite, bite. But so gently. He saw the image of his large tanned hands roving over her small white body, roving everywhere, before they settled on her throat, her white throat.

Her throat.

Wind soughed in the dark, giant trees, and the night that entered the car also entered Harry. There were whispers, snaking through and around the girl's heartbeat, skipping like stones over the incoming tide of his own pumping blood, and he reached for her. He wanted to be gentle, and he thought he was being gentle. Even after it was all over, he still believed that he'd been gentle.

It was only when Sly Jack Road stopped speaking to him that he realised its voice had ever been there at all. But by then, of course, it was too late. The evil had been set in motion, and it had attained its first claw-hold in the long struggle.

To come back.

The next thing Smooth Harry knew, his car was moving again, cruising through the neon wasteland of Eldritch's strip. Then he saw a blue light flashing in the Honda Accord's rear-view mirror...

Sam's fingers lifted from the keyboard and he felt the flow of power halted, as though an electrical circuit had been broken. He frowned at the screen, now filled with words, and wondered what had broken his concentration. Then he heard Jo softly calling his name. Before he had begun to write, the unexpected voice would probably have made him jump like a kangaroo. Now, simply because he had written something, all his fear and nervousness had evaporated, and it evoked nothing but mild surprise.

He swivelled around in his captain's chair. Jo was on the stairs, her head barely appearing above floor-level. She looked sheepish. There were a few tears in her eyes, and she was trying to smile. She looked human again.

'I've come to apologise.'

Sam nodded. She wouldn't have come back otherwise. 'Why don't you come up?'

She glanced at the monitor behind him. 'Are you working?'

'Yes. It's Eldritch time again.' Sam was amazed that he could announce this so calmly.

'Then I won't come up. But I'd like it if you came down. I mean, if you can, if you're not too busy...'

To show Jo there were no hard feelings, Sam put on a brief pantomime of frantically saving his work, as if he couldn't wait to join her. He heard her laugh a little, and thought that everything between them would be all right.

She waited for him on the stairs until he came, and then took him by the hand to lead him down to the first floor and into the bedroom where she had lit two aromatic candles, one either side of the bed. She swung the door shut behind them and grabbed Sam in a fierce embrace, which he responded to passionately. Her hand snaked around to the front of his jeans. They kissed almost hard enough to bruise.

'We could have been doing this all night,' Sam breathed into her mouth.

'Yes, but then you wouldn't have started the new book.'

Eventually, Jo sat him down on the end of the bed. 'We can't make love,' she said.

'No?'

'No. It's my time. That's why I've been in such a terrible mood, I suppose.'

'I would have been happy if we were just together,' Sam said. 'All that stuff earlier was just–'

'I know, I know. But shush now. *Shush'*

Jo let down her hair, which seemed to have regained its life, and it cascaded over her shoulders in rich, glossy waves. She knelt between Sam's thighs and gently pushed him onto his back.

'Just lie down.'

Sam closed his eyes as she began to fondle and stroke him through his jeans. After a few moments of divine pressure, she unbuckled his belt one-handed and then pulled down his pants. Her soft hand continued to stroke and roll, pull and tug, but then withdrew.

Sam opened his eyes to see what she was doing.

'Shush,' she said again. She lifted her sweater over her head and dropped it to the floor. Underneath, she was naked, her body magnificently heated. 'I'm going to take care of you now.'

Jo leaned forward between Sam's thighs, her heavy breasts mashing against his balls, and then bent her head to take him into her mouth.

Sam gasped. He reached out to hold her hair back so that he could see her face, and then abandoned himself to image locked to pure sensation, to a world where words didn't matter.

Other Works

Crime
(writing as PJ Shann)
The Queen of Hearts
Perfect Day
Perfect Peace
The Hunted Man 1: Old Dog New Trick
The Hunted Man 2: Identity Crisis
The Crime Short Story Collection

Horror
(writing as Jim Mullaney)
Comeback – a novel
The 1st Horror Short Story Collection
The 2nd Horror Short Story Collection

Please visit me at:
storiesneverend1.wordpress.com
or my **Amazon Authors Page**
or contact me at:
crimemysterysuspense@gmail.com

Thanks for Reading

37529542R00092

Printed in Poland
by Amazon Fulfillment
Poland Sp. z o.o., Wrocław